"Why did you do that?"

"Because I wished to," Christian said softly, his hand still tilting her face. "I have sunk into the despicable ways of the very wealthy. The habit of doing what I want is now firmly entrenched. I wanted to kiss you and I can still see no reason why I should not have followed my inclinations."

"How would you feel if I followed my inclinations and slapped your face hard?" Stephanie asked.

Patricia Wilson was born in Yorkshire, England, and lived there until she married and had four children. She loves traveling and has lived in Singapore, Africa and Spain. She had always wanted to be a writer but a growing family and a career as a teacher left her with little time to pursue her interest. With the encouragement of her family, she gave up teaching in order to concentrate on writing and her other interests of music and painting.

Books by Patricia Wilson

SENSE OF DESTINY
Patricia Wilson

Harlequin Books

TORONTO • NEW YORK • LONDON
AMSTERDAM • PARIS • SYDNEY • HAMBURG
STOCKHOLM • ATHENS • TOKYO • MILAN
MADRID • WARSAW • BUDAPEST • AUCKLAND

ISBN 0-373-03372-9

SENSE OF DESTINY

First North American Publication 1995.

Printed in U.S.A.

CHAPTER ONE

STEPHANIE could hear the phone ringing as she paid off the taxi and she almost fell up the steps in her haste to get to the front door. It wasn't easy, juggling with her luggage and trying to find the key, but the phone was still shrilling out as she managed to get into her flat and race across to pick it up. She was grateful that somebody had been persistent enough to keep on trying. It was good to have a phone call the moment she arrived back home. She would be able to catch up on the latest gossip and she was looking pleased as she lifted the receiver.

'Hello?' Stephanie had a happy voice, and her smile grew even wider as she heard who was calling.

'Stephanie! Where have you been? I've been ringing and ringing for *ages*!'

'I've only this minute got in through the door. I'm sorry I couldn't answer the phone from outside on the steps,' Stephanie laughed as she recognised the voice of her sister.

'I'm not talking about just now! I'm talking about days and days and days!'

'You know I've been away on an assignment. I did tell you before I went, Fiona.'

'I know, but I thought you would have been home long ago.'

Stephanie kicked off her boots and leaned back on the settee. The normally spoiled voice of her sister was more plaintive than usual and it was quite obvious that Fiona had rung up to ask a favour. Fiona had a strange way of asking favours; she started off in a bullying frame of mind and worked up to tears. Stephanie settled in. The call should take some time.

'Is anything wrong?' she enquired, trying to keep the amusement out of her voice.

'Nothing specifically,' Fiona said, her tone two shades more miserable. 'It's just that I wanted to get away from here. Thierry and I haven't been away alone for ages.'

'Well, just go! Who's to stop you?' As Stephanie put forward the suggestion, it did come to her mind that Thierry was not exactly his own boss. There was that big brother lurking away somewhere in the background.

'We can't take Jean-Paul with us and I've got absolutely *nobody* to look after him. It's all so impossible.' Fiona sighed tragically and it dawned on Stephanie then that she was being sized up for a job.

Not that she minded looking after Jean-Paul, not that she minded going out to the island. Her eyes strayed to the window where a flurry of snow was just sweeping past the pane. At the airport and then standing by the taxi she had been almost frozen to the bone. A couple of weeks on a sunny island would be rather nice.

'Oh! What a shame!' she commiserated. Stephanie carefully kept the eagerness out of her voice. It was never a good thing to let Fiona win easily. Besides, it was a sort of game. Fiona liked to feel that she made everyone toe the line when in actual fact they obeyed very readily, more often than not to save themselves from a performance of Fiona's pleading.

'Well, there are the servants, of course,' Fiona went on despairingly. 'I suppose I could leave him with those two but you know, Stephanie, that they're not to be trusted with a little boy and Jean-Paul is so very awkward when he wants to be.'

Stephanie shook her head in disbelief. Jean-Paul was no such thing. He was one of the sweetest children she had ever met, much sweeter than Fiona in actual fact. She ran it over in her mind, quite undecided as to how he had got like that with Fiona and Thierry as parents. Fiona had been spoiled as a child and had never stopped being spoiled. Thierry pampered her and so did everyone else. She insisted on being the queen bee and people made quite sure she was never inconvenienced. It just wasn't worth the bother it caused. Jean-Paul was one of those wondrous children who was impossible to spoil. He was gold all the way through.

She smiled at herself reminiscently as Fiona went on and on, complaining about how difficult things were, and while she talked Stephanie straightened her long, silver-blonde hair. It was a bit damp from being outside but she still had the tan she had acquired and she didn't much fancy losing it. She hadn't got any assignments at all as far as she could tell for quite a few weeks and she might as well spend that time out of England.

Her beautiful face was still glowing from her mad dash up the steps, colour under the golden tan, and her dark eyes were sparkling as usual, filled with fun.

'So you see,' Fiona ended frantically, 'if you don't come and rescue us, Thierry will have to go off by himself and I'll be left all alone and it's so *boring* here!'

Stephanie nodded wryly at the phone. Oh, yes, so very boring! A most beautiful house set almost on the beach on one of the most fabulous islands she had ever dreamed of in her whole life. Thierry was his own boss and answered only to his brother, who, as far as Stephanie knew, rarely appeared on the scene. It was true, he was a tyrant, that was well known, but he probably wasn't a tyrant to Thierry or to Fiona. If Fiona couldn't get round the monstrous big brother then nobody could.

Still, it was nothing to do with her—but she was dying to see Jean-Paul again. She hadn't seen him for two whole years. He would be seven now.

'Right! I give in,' she said briskly, her trained ear detecting that stage two was close, and she could do without the part where Fiona wept. 'When do you want me?'

'Oh, Stephanie! Can you really spare the time? Do you mean it? I feel so guilty—as if I'm putting upon you.'

Stephanie couldn't help laughing and she covered the phone with her hand. Fiona never changed. She had been like this as a child and she would always be like this.

'No, no. It's quite all right,' she managed soothingly. 'I have no assignments for quite a while and I'll be more than happy to come. In any case, I'm longing to see Jean-Paul again—and you and Thierry, of course.'

'Oh, we'll only be there for a little while when you arrive.' It was quite obvious that Fiona had it all planned and had fully expected that she would be able to get round her sister. 'We'll be nearly ready to go because there's no spare time. You know what Christian is like. If he wants Thierry somewhere he wants him there at once or even sooner.'

Happily, Stephanie did not know what Christian was like, except for the murmurs of complaint that came from Fiona. But then, Fiona complained about everything. Maybe he wasn't as bad as he sounded, although she *had* seen Thierry go white when he had been talking on the phone to his older brother.

She decided that it was time Fiona stopped talking. She had things to unpack and it looked as if she would be packing again in no time flat.

'Right! Let's have all the details,' she demanded, and Fiona changed her tone. Now she was brisk and cheerful, the weakling no longer needed, the plaintive sighs no longer necessary.

'So I'll see you as soon as possible,' she finished.

'Count on me,' Stephanie promised, grinning widely to herself.

She put the phone down and stood up, taking off her coat, collecting her boots and taking them through into

the bedroom. It was exhausting, listening to Fiona. All
she could hear now was silence and it made a nice change.
Her assignment had been rather noisy for a lot of the
time and she loved peace and quiet.

This was a pleasant flat, part of the house where she
had lived since she was a child. At one time it had been
a big house, a very special house, set in a quiet suburb
of London. It was still rather grand, with a long back
garden and high walls to protect it from prying neighbours, but now she shared it with other people.

After their parents died, she and Fiona had decided
to split the house up into flats. Fiona was already married
to a Frenchman who lived out in the French West Indies,
worked for his brother and was taking Fiona out there
with him. Now the only part of the house that Stephanie
could use was this ground-floor flat, although she and
Fiona still owned the whole building.

The flat was very comfortable, quite elegant and certainly big enough for her, and she did have the luxury
of having neighbours that she really liked. She was happy
here and happy with her job. Things were just about
perfect.

She glanced down and picked up a magazine and from
the front her own face looked back at her, the blonde
hair that was almost silvery, the dark eyes, the perfect
skin. Stephanie had been a top fashion model now for
a very long time and was often known as the Celestial
Girl because hers was the face that had launched the
new perfume and it was in every good magazine that
advertised the various products of the House of Celeste.

Not that anyone recognised her normally. She always
took good care to be herself and not her photographic
image when she was out in the street. She sighed contentedly. This last assignment had been good. She had
been out in the Canary Islands for several weeks and
everything had gone well. She had been modelling spring
clothes for several firms at once, the money was ex-

cellent and she had come back with quite a lot of booty because very often she was given some of the clothes she modelled.

Stephanie began to unpack her bags before she showered, carefully pulling out silk blouses with matching skirts and glowing summer cottons that had not yet reached the shops. She hung them up and looked them over with a very pleased eye. She could take a few of those with her and no need to buy anything new.

As she showered Stephanie's mind went skimming out to the island. She had not been there for a long time, nearly five years, but at the back of her mind it had remained a perfect place, a sort of paradise.

It was a dot on the blue-green of the Caribbean, perpetually sunny, cooled by the trade winds that blew all the year, and she remembered her first sight of it when she had gone to visit Fiona and Thierry. The steep hills were clothed in sugar cane and banana plantations, the small island dominated by a long-extinct volcano that added a dramatic finish to the greenery and the long golden sweep of shoreline. She could still see the palm trees that bent to the trade winds and in her mind she still heard the swell of the ocean on the Atlantic side of the island.

St Lucien was away from the main islands and had kept its unique atmosphere. It had been discovered by accident by French sailors in the early eighteenth century and they had named it after their captain when they had found, to their joy, that the water was plentiful and sweet and that fruit was there for the picking. It was a tiny part of France but in many ways it had never changed since Jules St Lucien's ship had sailed into the bay.

Stephanie had been nineteen when she had first gone out there for a long holiday and it had captivated her immediately. Jean-Paul had captivated her too and she could have stayed there for the rest of her life but her modelling career had swept her away and she had only been back once since then. Her time with her nephew had been time snatched in London when Fiona brought him over for holidays. Even so, they had developed a rapport that had not dimmed and she was as excited at the thought of seeing Jean-Paul again as she was at seeing the island.

She wondered if Christian Durand ever visited St Lucien or if he simply left things to Thierry. On her first visit she had expected him to arrive almost daily because his name seemed to be constantly on people's lips. Everyone on the island sang his praises. St Lucien might be a small part of France but Christian Durand seemed to own most of it. He owned the plantations, the harbour and the two small factories that gave work to the island people.

There had been talk of a grand hotel being built on the shore but he had crushed the idea at once. It was his island and he had money enough to back his decisions with power. He owned businesses all over the world and although he lived in Paris his power stretched a long way.

She had heard people talking, everyone in favour of his decisions, and it had given her shivers. At that time she had not been able to understand how Fiona dared to be married to Christian's brother and she had been very glad not to meet him, although she *almost* had.

On her last day there five years ago a great yacht had sailed into the bay to drop anchor in the deep blue waters and Stephanie had been fascinated. Watching it through Thierry's binoculars, she had called excitedly for Fiona to come and look but Fiona hadn't been excited at all.

'It's Christian,' she said worriedly. 'We didn't expect him for a week. I wonder why he's come early?'

'You have forgotten the date, *chérie*,' Thierry informed her, coming on to the veranda and putting an arm around his wife. 'It is Christian's birthday in two days and he always comes home.'

'Were you born here?' Stephanie looked round in surprise and Thierry grinned at her.

'I was born in Paris, *ma chère*. Christian was born here and he always comes back on his birthday no matter where he is or what is happening. He will have brought friends and in two days there will be fireworks and plenty of lights on that yacht. You should stay and join us. It is time you met my big brother.'

Stephanie smiled and went back to watching the beautiful boat, thankful that she was leaving. The thought of meeting Christian Durand gave her more shivers than she had ever had before. She was impressed by his tremendous power and he didn't sound at all merry and easygoing like Thierry.

As she watched, a tall, dark-haired man came on deck. He was wearing white jeans and a black shirt and he moved lithely across to the rails, his eyes obviously trained on the house. It was too far away for her really to see him well but his hair seemed to be as black as the shirt he wore and even from that distance she could see how tanned he was.

Thierry saw him too and touched her shoulder.

'Christian,' he pointed out but she had already fathomed that out. She couldn't take her eyes away from him and she felt flustered and scared. She was praying he would give her time to leave before he visited. Luckily, he did.

She dried herself, glancing in the mirror and smiling. She was not now an anxious nineteen-year-old girl. She could tackle Christian Durand with one hand tied behind her back. Anyway, he wouldn't come. Thierry would be away and as far as she could remember it was nobody's birthday at all.

Stephanie sat in the garden, her long brown legs stretched out in front of her. The weather was perfect. Her eyes were shielded by sunglasses but she could still see how the green lawn stretched down to the edge of a very low cliff where wide steps led to the beach. The soft wind blew her hair, cooling her skin and making gentle sounds through the palms and flowering bushes that edged the wide lawns.

Across the bay was a deserted blue cove, ringed by low mountains, their slopes green and cool. There were no houses on that side of the bay but often boats moored there, looking like white swans on a blue sea. It was beautiful, the most beautiful place she had ever seen, and right now she never wanted to leave.

Stephanie had been on the island for two days. Jean-Paul had been ecstatic to see her, the servants had greeted her like an old friend and the morning after her arrival Fiona and Thierry had left. Christian wanted Thierry to go to Canada but before then they had planned a secret holiday alone and Stephanie assumed that Christian Durand knew nothing about it. Certainly Fiona had seemed a trifle nervous, anxious to be off, as if she expected big brother suddenly to appear over her shoulder. It had amused Stephanie because Fiona was more accustomed to creating attacks of nerves than feeling them herself. Christian Durand must be *some* tyrant.

She had found out how much of a tyrant he was on the evening before Fiona and Thierry left, and Stephanie's smiles had died as indignation took their place.

'We've got to get away for a while, right away,' Fiona had told her. Stephanie had been unpacking and Fiona had come to sit on the bed, none of her usual spoiled looks about her. 'I have to get Thierry out of Christian's clutches.'

'You mean he's going to strike out on his own?' Stephanie asked, abandoning her packing to sit and listen carefully.

'No.' Fiona grimaced and looked up with real worry on her face. 'I wish he could but that's impossible. All he needs to do is stand up to Christian more and, as things are, he's not about to do that.'

Stephanie looked at her sister closely. She knew Fiona's ways. There was always some plot hatching and this was probably another.

'You seem to have a pretty good life here,' she ventured. 'Thierry is just about the easiest person in the world to get on with and Christian is a long way off when you come to look at it.'

'Christian is right at the end of a telephone!' Fiona stated sharply. 'And it's Thierry's easygoing ways that make things simple for Christian. He dictates every aspect of our lives. He *interferes*, Stephanie, and now he's gone too far. I can't ignore it any longer.'

She looked very upset and very determined and she wasn't wheedling either. Stephanie settled down with interest.

'What has big brother done now?' she asked quietly.

'He's taking Jean-Paul away from us.' Fiona's dejection convinced Stephanie immediately and her heart gave an anxious little leap.

'What do you mean? He can't! Jean-Paul is your son. No uncle can just whisk him away as if you didn't exist.'

'Christian is much more subtle than that,' Fiona said bitterly. 'It's all for Jean-Paul's good, you see—on the face of it. Jean-Paul is to be educated in Paris, under Christian's care. We are to stay here. You can see the plan, can't you, Stephanie? Give it a few years and he'll be more like Christian than Thierry. Gradually, we'll lose him.'

Yes, Stephanie could see the plan. Educate Jean-Paul in Paris with Christian supervising his life, introducing him into the business, eventually making him more responsible. Jean-Paul would grow up just like his uncle. A few years and he would be Christian Durand mark two; the wonderful little boy he was now would be submerged and lost.

'Right! What are we going to do?' she demanded fiercely, her blood boiling at the injustice of it, to say nothing of the high-handed arrangement.

'I'm getting Thierry away where I can talk to him without any influence from Christian,' Fiona said firmly. 'There'll be no telephone calls, no letters. By the time we come back he'll be different and he'll see how things really are. He'll tackle Christian then, believe me!'

Stephanie did. Fiona, undiluted, could move mountains and melt rocks.

'It's such a relief to know that you're in this with me,' Fiona stated, jumping up to hug her, and Stephanie had a momentary qualm. She felt like sniffing the air suspiciously. Being 'in' something with Fiona was worrying but there was no getting away from the fact that Christian Durand was planning Jean-Paul's life around himself. They would all lose a dear little boy and he would be lost forever. Seeing him again had only made her more sure of her love for him. Fiona was right, she *was* in this.

'Where are you going?' she asked intently, and Fiona closed up at once.

'Just don't ask,' she begged. 'I know Jean-Paul is safe here with you on the island. It's better that you don't know our exact location—just somewhere in Canada. It's only for a week after all and then we'll be back to doing Christian's bidding. If he should phone, or, worse still, if he should come, he would get our address from you right away.'

'No chance!' Stephanie said sharply. 'He doesn't scare me.'

'You don't know him,' Fiona reminded her gloomily. 'He's far above ordinary people like us. You'd crumble, Stephanie—even you.'

Stephanie had begged to differ but she'd said nothing more. It sounded like a good plan and she was quite prepared to take the responsibility while they were away. She'd agreed and Fiona had looked much more settled about things.

Now they were gone and it seemed that the entire household had breathed a sigh of relief at the departure because Fiona was as irritating when packing clothes as she was when she was making other people do her bidding. When they'd left there was just contentment and peace.

Stephanie leaned back, smiling at the blue sky. This was the way to live. Of course, she could now understand Fiona's air of disillusionment. There was a serpent in this particular paradise. Her smile turned to a frown. Christian Durand was quite clearly a megalomaniac.

Jean-Paul came running across the garden and sat down on the grass beside her.

'It's a beautiful day,' he volunteered, and Stephanie's smile came back as she glanced down at him. He was a handsome little boy, dark-haired and dark-eyed, very much like Thierry. He must stay like that and she would see to it that he did. Christian Durand could just mind his own business.

'It's all of that,' she agreed, but Jean-Paul had more on his mind.

'We shall have to try and find something to do.' He made this remark rather wistfully and Stephanie smiled even more broadly. He was up to something, she knew that quite well but she didn't really mind. He was never in serious mischief.

'When you came here before, I was very small,' he pointed out when she said nothing at all.

'You were. Two years old, in fact.'

'You were a lot younger too,' Jean-Paul continued, and Stephanie gave a tragic sigh.

'Yes. I'm getting old now. It comes to everybody in the end.'

Jean-Paul looked up at her in a startled manner, searching for laughter and finding none although it took a great effort to keep her face straight.

'When he knew you were coming, Papa said you were perfect,' he informed her urgently, no doubt worried by her rapid descent into old age.

'That was very nice of him,' Stephanie conceded. 'I expect he meant that my timing was perfect, arriving here just ready for them to leave.'

'Oh, no, no! He meant you were beautiful. I'm sure he meant that,' Jean-Paul said firmly and Stephanie shook her head in amusement. He was much more French than English but his mother's wheedling ways had not escaped him, although he went about things in a much more diplomatic manner. She knew all this was leading somewhere. She hadn't spent her childhood with Fiona for nothing.

She kept quiet, however, and presently Jean-Paul flung himself back on the grass, staring at the high blue sky.

'Next year I shall go to school in France,' he informed her.

Stephanie sat up straight, took off her sunglasses and stared down at him, trying to gauge how he was taking this.

'So I hear. You'll be in Paris.'

'Yes. Oncle Christian has arranged it all. It is the school that Papa went to and I will be a day boy. I'll stay with Oncle Christian. He will look after me and I will go to school from his house.'

'Yes,' Stephanie murmured. 'Uncle Christian arranged everything as you said.'

'He did. It was very good of him. Maman said so.'

Stephanie leaned back, thinking about it. She supposed that Jean-Paul really could not continue to stay on the island. Now that he was seven he needed a more

French education in a more sophisticated place. She saw the need for that but the fact was that Christian Durand could have transferred Thierry to Paris. He must have hundreds of underlings who could come out here.

Fiona was right. He was taking a strong grip on Jean-Paul at an early age, moulding him into his own image. Her mind went back to the first time she had seen Christian Durand and she wondered what he looked like now, probably even more forbidding, richer, older and more domineering. She knew that time had made him more powerful but it had also made her more sure of herself and she could now afford to ignore him if they should meet. Her shyness had vanished.

He had to be stopped and she would help Fiona to stop him. She could well imagine that with Jean-Paul in Paris she would never see him at all, close though he would be. She would have to cross swords with Christian Durand in order to be able to get to her nephew, and he would try to stop her, she was sure of that. It would have been a good deal better if 'Oncle Christian' had married and raised his own family instead of interfering in his brother's affairs.

Jean-Paul interrupted her thoughts.

'It's easy to get very bored on St Lucien,' he complained quietly. 'I shall be very bored—tomorrow.'

Stephanie began to laugh. Now they were coming to it. She should have known better than to be side-tracked; a little bit of Fiona was really etched deep inside him.

'And why will you be particularly bored tomorrow?' she enquired, and she got a sigh that really reminded her of her sister.

'There is going to be a fair in the village but I don't expect I will be allowed to go.' He said that with a quick little glance at her and Stephanie decided to play it straight down the line.

'I can't see why not. I'm quite prepared to take you,' she offered, but it was not enough apparently.

'Ah! But you see, there's a fancy-dress competition and I haven't got a fancy-dress costume. I would look foolish.' He sat up, folding his hands on his knees, resting his chin on them and looking very gloomy. Stephanie realised they had reached the point of the whole matter: she was to make him a costume.

'Have you had any thoughts about it?' she asked, and he shook his head.

'No, but Louisa has and I don't like her thoughts at all.'

'What were her thoughts about?' Stephanie could understand his misgivings. Louisa had been with the household for a very long time. She was fat and jolly, given to going into great fits of loud laughter, and her ideas were often bizarre.

'She wanted to put me into a long gown with beads. She was going to paint my face.'

'Not a good idea,' Stephanie managed seriously, shaking her head as her nephew watched her anxiously.

'Louisa says there's nothing else in the house.'

'We'll look.' Stephanie jumped up and took his hand and together they marched into the house. It was all very amusing. She was sure that any other child would have run out to her and asked outright for a fancy-dress costume. This was Fiona's child, though, and he had given her a long detour before coming to the point.

Honour was at stake and she had to come up with something that did not include beads and a long gown and certainly not painting the face. By the end of the afternoon, Stephanie sat with Louisa on the veranda, sewing frantically. They had gathered all sorts of scraps of material and Jean-Paul stayed around for the many fittings. He never had one word of complaint and just before dinner they had completed their task.

A large piece of bright red material, shaped and padded with cardboard, went over his head. It was fat and round with tufts of green at the neck. He had to

have a skirt but it was not the sort of skirt that Louisa
had thought of. It was bright green with pieces of yellow
and that too had been stiffened. With the addition of
other bits and pieces, Stephanie declared herself to be
satisfied and took Jean-Paul indoors to view himself in
one of the long bathroom mirrors.

'What do you think?'

She stood back and he turned slowly to admire himself.

'It's very good! I am a tomato!'

'You're much more than that,' Stephanie pointed out
triumphantly. 'You're a salad. It's sure to win a prize.'

'Oh, thank you, Tante Stephanie! You're wonderful.
Papa is right. You are perfect.'

'But you're not,' Stephanie pointed out with a mocking
frown on her face. 'You've forgotten twice already.'

He laughed and then gave her a hug.

'Tante Stephanie makes you feel old and you are
already twenty-four.'

'Too true,' Stephanie sighed and he giggled happily.

'I will not forget again,' he promised.

Later, when Jean-Paul went to bed, his costume was
beside him on a chair and as Stephanie put out the light
he closed his eyes contentedly.

'Goodnight, Stevie,' he murmured.

She kissed his cheek and smiled to herself. This was
what a little boy needed, not some tyrant hovering over
him. They could manage very well without Christian
Durand.

They left for the village immediately after lunch,
Stephanie driving the Jeep that Thierry used for trips
around the island and Jean-Paul sitting like a mouse,
protecting his costume from creases.

It was another wonderful day. Stephanie wore white
shorts and a red shirt. Her long silvery hair was tied in
a loose knot and pulled over her shoulder. Inside she
felt about nineteen again, or even younger than that,

and she knew it was the effect of the sunlight and the company of a little boy who still found magic in things. It was how she felt herself and at the moment there was nothing but magic on St Lucien. She would keep it like that for Jean-Paul.

The fair was an excuse to make music, have a market and dance in the streets and Stephanie loved it. Tourists came to the island and she saw plenty of white faces but mostly she was happy with the good-natured people who lived here and accepted her when they recognised her small companion.

He did not win first prize but they had to agree that it would have been impossible. The first prize went to a king who was on stilts and Jean-Paul would not have been able to manage that. He won second prize, though, and it was with a very contented charge beside her that Stephanie turned the Jeep for home as the day drew to a close. She felt almost as tired as Jean-Paul looked.

She drove quickly through the narrow lanes to the house, both of them singing loudly, but as they drew up in front of the long white veranda the smile died on Stephanie's face. Louisa was hanging about looking anxious and she went rapidly away at the sound of a sharp command, her round eyes regarding Stephanie with pity.

Stephanie knew there was trouble at once because a tall, dark-haired man strode out from the lighted house to meet them with a thunderous look about him that threatened trouble. After one swift glance at Jean-Paul, he turned all his attention to Stephanie in a savage way that stunned her and she sat in the Jeep looking up at him as he stood on the veranda steps.

She knew instantly who this was but she had not quite expected him to be so tall, so powerful or so angry. She hadn't expected to find brilliantly blue eyes turned on her with murderous intent either. Thierry's eyes were dark, normal, but Christian Durand had eyes like blue laser beams and they were cutting her to pieces immediately.

He was towering over her, taking her by surprise, his handsome face so furious that she couldn't get a word out. Her suppositions had been correct. He *was* older, more powerful and he was certainly forbidding.

Even Jean-Paul was stunned, but not for long.

'Oncle Christian!' He sprang out of the car and after one startled glance at his nephew's appearance Christian's blue eyes softened into a smile.

'And where have you been, *mon ami*?' he enquired softly. He bent to hug Jean-Paul, carefully avoiding crushing his costume, and Stephanie gave him a few marks for that but they were very low marks indeed. He looked like a fierce marauder and he was here to get to Jean-Paul immediately.

'I've been to the fair!' Jean-Paul told him excitedly, ignoring in his innocence the signs of seething rage that had not gone away. 'I won second prize!' He waved his card but already the blue eyes were back to mutilating Stephanie, the black brows drawn together in a terrifying frown.

'You took my nephew to the village?' he asked in a soft, menacing voice. She had climbed out of the Jeep and his eyes raked over her angrily, noting the shorts and her long legs, the silky hair tied back in a knot. 'You are not even old enough to take care of yourself! My brother left a young girl in charge of his son and the moment they are gone you go racing off to the village without permission? Whatever he has promised I will pay now. Jean-Paul is my affair. You may go back to your holiday villa and rejoin your parents!'

CHAPTER TWO

STEPHANIE'S mouth opened in outrage and her dark eyes sparkled with resentment. Nobody had ever spoken to her like that in her whole life and she wasn't taking it now!

'But Stevie didn't need permission, Oncle Christian,' Jean-Paul said hurriedly before Stephanie could gather any acid words together. 'Stevie is in charge of the house until Maman and Papa return. Papa said so and he told Louisa quite loudly so that she would not forget.'

'You may go inside, Jean-Paul,' Christian said firmly. 'I will deal with this. It is not suitable for someone so young to look after you when your parents are away. It is also not suitable for her to drive.'

'I don't think you understand, Oncle Christian,' Jean-Paul insisted anxiously. 'Stevie is not young. She is quite old. She is twenty-four and also she is my aunt.'

Stephanie had to agree she couldn't have done better herself without resorting to the violence that was right at the top of her mind, because Christian Durand simply froze. Slowly he turned and looked her over and she could see he hadn't changed his mind about her at all. It even seemed he was doubting Jean-Paul's words.

'Is this true? You are Fiona's sister, Stephanie Caine?' he asked coldly.

'I am!' She turned dark eyes on him that matched his annoyance. 'It's the only way I could become Jean-Paul's aunt without being related to you. Naturally it was the way I chose, being filled with the urge to preserve my sanity!'

23

'I apologise, *mademoiselle*,' he said stiffly but she noted that his expression did not match the words. He was still furiously angry and very suspicious of her but Jean-Paul had relaxed. The introductions were completed and he didn't understand the finer points of Stephanie's insult.

'Stevie made my costume and I won second prize,' he pointed out again. 'I am a salad, Oncle Christian.'

'Yes. I can see that.' Stephanie could see that Christian Durand was hanging on to his temper by a very thin thread. He also looked as if he had inadvertently stepped into a lunatic world and she assumed that he attributed that to her. 'Perhaps you had better change into something different?' he advised and it was clear that he wanted the boy out of the way so that he could savage Stephanie further. He had attacked her on sight with no show of diplomacy. He was, as she had always imagined, a monster. He certainly looked the part and she wondered how he would react if she informed him that she knew all about his plans and meant to stop him.

'Will you help me, Stevie?' Jean-Paul appealed to her but before she could move Christian had taken over again.

'I wish to speak privately to your aunt Stephanie. No doubt she will join you in a little while.'

Jean-Paul hesitated but finally went. Not even a grown-up could have defied Christian Durand and it was certainly not possible for a small boy to defy him. As Jean-Paul left, Stephanie steeled herself for trouble and it came fast.

'I apologise for speaking to you as I did, *mademoiselle*,' he said curtly. 'Obviously I did not know that you were Fiona's sister. However, it does not change the situation. Jean-Paul is not to be allowed to go into the village at all. I will remain here in any case until my brother and his wife return. The responsibility therefore no longer rests with you.'

The great take-over! What did he intend to do, remove Jean-Paul and take him to Paris now before Fiona came back? It was not beyond the bounds of possibility and she could just imagine him saying that he had come and found Jean-Paul alone and unsupervised.

'Fiona and Thierry handed Jean-Paul over to me,' Stephanie said hotly, turning on him with flashing dark eyes. 'I intend to look after him until they come back. You may own all you survey, Monsieur Durand, but you most certainly do not own Jean-Paul. You are his uncle and I am his aunt. That makes us equal even though you seem to think you have some superior claim. I can well imagine what a happy time he'll have, with you forbidding him to do just about everything. There's no way you're giving me my marching orders so forget all about it.'

He looked so astonished at her attack that had she not been so angry Stephanie would have laughed.

'I do not entirely understand you, Mademoiselle Caine,' he grated, pinning her with brilliant eyes, 'although I certainly follow the trend of your remarks. I am not sending you away. You may stay here and have a holiday. However, I am here too and I will control the situation. I have brought a friend with me who will assist me in looking after Jean-Paul.'

Before Stephanie could answer a woman walked on to the veranda and she could see exactly what sort of a friend this was. She was tall and very good-looking, her dark hair long and beautifully arranged. With the perfect make-up, the glossy lips and her sophisticated clothes she seemed to be straight from Paris and she did not look the sort of person who would be at all interested in Jean-Paul's happiness.

She stared at Stephanie, not impressed by her shorts and shirt or by her wind-tossed hair.

'This is Madame Pascal,' Christian introduced. 'Denise has children of her own.'

Stephanie could see that this fact gave Madame Pascal a certain edge. She did not look as if she would take kindly to children, however, and there was no way she was looking after Jean-Paul. Still, it was not this woman's fault that Christian Durand was an imperious dictator. He had probably ordered her to help and Stephanie prided herself on her scrupulous fairness.

'How do you do?' Stephanie murmured politely but it was almost ignored. All she got was a brief nod before she was dismissed as being unimportant. Obviously she was as bad as her escort and Stephanie reorganised her thoughts. It was two to one by the look of things.

'Could I have one of those maids to help me unpack, Christian?' Ignoring Stephanie completely, Denise Pascal turned a brilliant smile on him and he was instantly pleasant.

'Of course, Denise. If you care to go to your room I'll send one of them up to you.' As she went, he turned to Stephanie. 'As you can see, you may have a relaxed holiday,' he assured her coldly. 'Denise and I will manage Jean-Paul with no trouble.'

'Over my dead body! You're certainly going to have trouble because *I'm* here to take care of Jean-Paul,' Stephanie snapped, 'and I'm staying to do just that!' She had seen the candidate for her position and she was not at all impressed. She looked up at him defiantly. 'I'd like to know how you're going to stop me from doing what his mother and father asked.'

'I can put you on a plane, *mademoiselle*,' he suggested menacingly, and she smiled up into his narrowed blue eyes.

'Like a suitcase? I'm not inanimate, I would resist. In any case, I rather think you would then have a rebellion on your hands. Jean-Paul wouldn't take kindly to it. I'm his favourite aunt and although he's the sweetest boy in the world he *is* Fiona's son!'

For a few seconds he stared down at her angrily and then a rather sardonic smile twisted his lips.

'No doubt we will come to some arrangement,' he murmured drily. 'We will leave it for now. Perhaps you had better go and prepare for dinner, Mademoiselle Caine.' His eyes skimmed over her slender figure and noted the shorts again. She could see that she compared badly with Denise Pascal but she wasn't at all put out.

'Please understand that you will not order me about in any way at all,' she said sharply and the sardonic smile grew.

'I do not intend to do that, *mademoiselle*,' he murmured silkily. 'Dress for dinner or do not, as you wish. In any case, I imagined you were anxious to see to Jean-Paul? He would be most uncomfortable eating in his costume. If you do not intend to prepare for dinner yourself, perhaps you should go and prepare your salad for his meal?'

Stephanie glared at him and marched off. Just who did he think he was, coming here and taking over like a king? He didn't own Jean-Paul. If she left him to the mercy of his uncle Christian and that woman she would never be able to sleep. By the time Fiona and Thierry came back, Jean-Paul would be changed, probably even cowed—*if* he was still permitted to be here! Just let them try to interfere.

She flatly refused to dress up for dinner too. She had a shower after she had seen to Jean-Paul but as time was pressing it was a very hurried shower. All she managed with make-up was a quick dab at her nose with powder and an equally quick covering of lip-gloss on her mouth. She picked out her most comfortable cotton dress and brushed her hair.

Almost as a challenge, she left it long and fastened in the loose knot again. If he thought she looked like a teenager he was going to find out how awkward a teenager could be. She collected Jean-Paul and marched down to dinner, not at all surprised that Denise Pascal had not yet put in an appearance.

Before Christian could offer her a drink, Stephanie poured one for herself to prove her equal status and he looked disgusted. She supposed it was less than feminine but she was not going to let him take over in any way at all and he might as well know it right away. She was Jean-Paul's aunt, she had been invited here and she was already established in the house.

He slanted a frosty look at her with those blue eyes and noted her bare legs and long hair.

'Perhaps I can be forgiven for thinking you were very young,' he murmured, his glance taking in the swirling cotton dress that left her brown shoulders uncovered. Stephanie took it to be an insolent look and her dark eyes flashed at him.

'I would imagine you find it easy to forgive yourself almost anything,' she pronounced. 'Therefore, I'll keep out of it altogether and let you get on with it.'

'Courtesy is a necessity of life,' he rasped and she glanced at him in mock-astonishment.

'You read all that while I was getting changed? I was only a few minutes, too. Perhaps you'll remember it the next time you meet a complete stranger, Monsieur Durand.'

His reply was going to be very caustic, she could see that, but right on cue Denise entered the room and Stephanie saw that she had decided that dressing for dinner was important. She had to admit that the dress the dark-haired woman wore was stunning. Denise was well aware of her own beauty and she cast a dismissive look at Stephanie, counting her as no opposition at all. She did not like the idea of having Jean-Paul there, however.

'Does the child normally dine with the adults, Christian?' she asked sweetly. 'Surely he would be better having his meal separately and going to bed? My own children always did this. It is not good for children to be up late.' From her look it seemed that she was doubtful about Stephanie being there too. Jean-Paul looked downcast and Stephanie intervened before Christian could reply.

'In the absence of his father,' she pointed out sharply, 'Jean-Paul is our host. It's perhaps a little too much for him on this occasion but I hardly think it would be polite to banish him to his room. Courtesy, after all, is a necessity of life.'

Christian said nothing but she saw by the way his lips tightened and by the look he shot her that his opinion of her had slipped one more notch. It didn't bother her at all. She would hold her own with these two and see to it that Jean-Paul didn't suffer from their interference. His life would be intolerable if she went away and she had no intention of being edged out. If they wanted a battle she could give them one. In fact she could give them one each.

'So you are Jean-Paul's aunt, Mademoiselle Caine?' Denise purred during dinner. 'You must be much younger than your sister.'

Stephanie bridled at the dismissive tone. They had been discussing her, it seemed, no doubt talking in shocked voices about her unsuitability as a companion for Jean-Paul.

'Not much younger,' she assured Denise sweetly. 'Obviously you've never met my sister. In my family we age very slowly; it's in the genes, you know.'

Beneath Denise's smooth curves there was a tendency to plumpness and the barb struck home. Her face flushed and she pinned Stephanie with angry eyes. So did Christian.

'I have never found that chronological age makes a woman, *mademoiselle*,' he said coldly. 'There is a certain mystical something, a warmth, an instinctive ability to act wisely, in a real woman. That is also in the genes, I imagine?'

Stephanie took the point. She had behaved irresponsibly according to the powerful Monsieur Durand—so had Fiona in going off with her husband and leaving a scatter-brain in charge. For the moment she couldn't think of a suitably acid reply and Denise glowed.

'I hope you find me a real woman, *chéri*?' she asked with a lingering glance at him and he smiled down at her in what Stephanie considered to be a most disgraceful way, taking into account that Jean-Paul was there.

'Have I ever given you any reason to doubt it?' he asked softly.

It was quite sickening and Stephanie was heartily glad when the meal ended.

'What do you think of Madame Pascal?' Jean-Paul asked quietly as she put him to bed later.

'Yuk!' Stephanie said and he looked up at her carefully.

'Is that bad?'

'Bad enough,' she assured him. 'We'll just ignore her, shall we?'

'I hope she goes away,' he muttered sleepily. 'I just want you and Oncle Christian.'

Stephanie nodded sympathetically and kept her thoughts to herself. It would not do to give her opinion of Uncle Christian. Jean-Paul was clearly fond of him, though why she couldn't understand. He was the hardest man she had ever had the misfortune to meet and he was obviously power-mad. His tough good looks covered ferocity and those blue eyes raking over her made her feel uncomfortable. All her peace was gone.

It was interesting that Christian had not brought up the subject of Jean-Paul's schooling. That would have been a very good ace to play and yet he had said nothing.

He had merely concentrated on getting Jean-Paul to himself so far. In all probability, Denise Pascal was here to look things over. If she lived with Christian in Paris then she too was going to be involved with Jean-Paul's future.

The idea was atrocious. They had to be stopped and although she could not do anything about that particular plan she could hold the fort here until Fiona worked something out. No way were they getting rid of her!

Next morning Stephanie was awakened by Jean-Paul racing in to bounce on her bed. He had never done that before but today, apparently, he was exuberant.

'It's a wonderful day!' he cried, landing dangerously close to her head. When she tried to hide he bounced even more and she had to come out and defend herself.

'Fiend!' Stephanie shouted, taking her pillow and beating him about the back. She knelt up in bed and pulled him out from his refuge under the sheets, attacking him wildly as he screamed with laughter. 'Surrender!' she commanded and he fell on his back, protecting his face as she hovered over him.

'I will never surrender,' he laughed. 'The Durands never give in!'

'Then it's to the death!' Stephanie declared, raising the pillow for another attack.

She glanced up as a movement caught her eye and Christian was standing outside the open door, leaning against the wall. Obviously Jean-Paul had just rushed in to spring on her and had left the door open. Now their antics were providing interesting viewing for the wicked uncle who watched and said absolutely nothing. The brilliant blue eyes ranged over Stephanie minutely and she knelt there with the pillow half raised, frozen into immobility by the intent, assessing look.

A shiver of awareness ran down her spine as she stared back at the tall, athletic figure. There was a taut, muscular power to his body. He stood perfectly still as if every one of his senses was given up to watching her and she couldn't look away from him.

'Oh, Oncle Christian.' Jean-Paul had realised that Stephanie was silent and he rolled over to look. 'It's a wonderful day!'

'If you survive it,' Christian agreed. 'Perhaps you should surrender and leave Aunt Stephanie in peace. She needs to dress.'

It was a remark aimed deliberately at Stephanie because although he was speaking to his nephew Christian never let his eyes move from her and she realised she was providing quite a spectacle. Her nightie was a short white silky creation with more lace than substance. It was little more than a camisole top with matching panties and at the moment she was all legs, tousled blonde hair and wide, dark eyes that were beginning to look furious.

'Pardon me.' Jean-Paul leapt obediently from the bed and moved to the door. 'I did not think. I am dressed, you see.'

'I noticed,' Christian remarked very softly. 'Shall we go to breakfast?' His eyes slanted over Stephanie's flushed face as he took charge of Jean-Paul and closed the door slowly.

Stephanie sprang off the bed in a rage. She had let him mesmerise her. She had said nothing at all. Round one to the opposition! She was flushed with embarrassment after that look but she was too furious to let it linger in her mind. While she was up here getting dressed, Christian Durand would be laying down the law to Jean-Paul and persuading him that it would be better to stay indoors than to do anything else.

She rushed under the shower and dressed with a great deal of speed. Any of her photographers would have been proud of her. They would have wanted a bit more polish than she gave herself, however, but it was not possible to be in two places at once and she knew exactly where she was going immediately. If Uncle Christian wanted to stick close to his nephew he would have to push himself in between them and she intended to leave no room at all.

They were having breakfast as she came into the room and they both rose politely. Stephanie cast a quick look at Jean-Paul and was relieved to see that he didn't yet look subdued. Rescue had arrived in time. Denise Pascal was not there. She would be lingering in bed, of course, and as far as Stephanie could see that was exactly what she would have been doing had she been allowed to take care of Jean-Paul. Luckily, *she* was here to see to things.

'You were very quick, Stevie,' Jean-Paul observed as she sat to eat her breakfast.

'I didn't want to miss anything,' she assured him, glancing malevolently at Christian whose blue eyes were relentlessly on her. She saw his lips twist wryly before he said,

'It would be more polite to call your aunt by her proper title, Jean-Paul. She is grown-up and surely wishes to be called Aunt Stephanie?'

'She will be very cross if I call her that,' Jean-Paul assured him seriously. 'I have always called her Stevie. She was very young when she came here before but now that she is old she likes to stay with her younger name. I know she would like it if you called her Stevie too,' he added hopefully with a quick glance at Stephanie's face.

She wasn't looking as if she liked anything at that moment. Now the interfering uncle was laying down rules about her name! She glared at Christian and he looked back at her sardonically, his eyes flashing over her silvery hair as if it astonished him.

'It is a nickname,' he pointed out to Jean-Paul. 'A nickname is an affectionate way of speaking to people you care about. I do not know your aunt well enough.'

'When you get to know her you can call her Stevie,' Jean-Paul decided comfortably, getting on with his meal. 'It won't take long.'

'About a millennium,' Stephanie muttered and Christian fixed her with blue eyes that had hardened to ice.

'*D'accord,*' he snapped. 'Not long at all, in the circumstances.'

Stephanie didn't care. She was immune to blue-eyed annihilation and she began to speak to Jean-Paul as if there were just the two of them there. It was easy because they had the success of their fancy-dress parade to discuss and Christian could not enter the conversation unless he was invited. Jean-Paul was too excited to remember and Stephanie was determined to keep him out of things.

In the end he quietly excused himself and left, looking very impatient with both of them, and she grinned to herself as she watched him go. She wasn't going to let good manners get in her way. This was a battle and she rather felt she had taken the second round easily.

Christian went on to the veranda and she watched him surreptitiously. He moved like an athlete, his dark hair catching the sunlight as he walked to the edge of the lawn and looked down on the beach and she had the feeling that he was a little taken aback at her refusal to bend the knee. She could understand that. He was important, a big name and very wealthy. Defiance would no doubt astonish him. If she had been easily scared he would have been a bit too much for her, but she wasn't easily scared.

When she had secretly observed him five years ago as he had stood on the deck of his splendid yacht she had felt that he looked relaxed and calm, the sort of man who would be tolerant or even indulgent. It was not fear of his temper that had made her want to escape before he arrived—she had not wanted to face such forceful

masculinity. Now he looked anything but calm and he
certainly didn't look indulgent. He appeared to be
irritated beyond words and there was a watchful look
about him even when he was not facing her.

It didn't matter. She intended to carry out her plans.
Christian and his companion could do exactly as they
wished, providing they did not get in her way. What she
would do if he attempted to take Jean-Paul away to Paris
she did not know and for the first time she wished she
had insisted on Fiona giving her a forwarding address.
It was too late now, though. She would have to play this
by ear.

'What shall we do today?' she asked as Jean-Paul
began to look around and take no more interest in food.

'We could all go to the cove.' He looked at her brightly
and Stephanie eyed him sternly.

'All?' she enquired with raised brows and he grimaced
as he followed her thoughts.

'If Oncle Christian comes we will have to invite
Madame Pascal also?' he asked, looking as if he hoped
she would say no.

'I'm afraid so,' Stephanie assured him. 'It would be
quite rude to leave Madame Pascal here alone while we
went off to enjoy ourselves.'

Not that Denise would want to swim, she mused
silently. The well groomed hair would become wet, so
would the face. She kept the thought to herself. Christian
looked as if he could swim any distance, any time, and
she wasn't about to give him the chance to join them.
In any case, he would probably forbid any such
expedition.

'Let's just go alone,' she wheedled. 'We can take a
packed lunch and we can climb down to the cove and
stay all day.'

'*D'accord*!' Jean-Paul agreed, just like his aloof uncle,
and Stephanie hid her disappointment at this sign of
French blood. When she had him to herself she would

bring out the English in him. She went off to order their lunch and told Louisa most firmly that it was a secret. If sneaking off was a necessity, then she would sneak off.

They made it without any problem because Christian had disappeared when she came back to collect Jean-Paul. She went on to the veranda to search carefully with narrowed eyes but he was nowhere to be seen and Stephanie snorted with annoyance. One guardian off on his own affairs and the other still in bed. It was a good job she was here, otherwise Jean-Paul would have been totally neglected. He would be a very lonely little boy if he went to live in Paris with Christian.

From the house, the cove with its green-clad mountains looked quite close but Stephanie knew it was a good way off. She had been there before on her previous visit and although that had been a long time ago she had not forgotten that a fairly good road ran partly down to the sea. It still left a long climb down and up again but the road was quite accessible to the Jeep and, as to the distance, she rather thought it would be a good idea to be well out of reach of Christian Durand. He might have disappeared but it was certainly only for the time being. His determination to rule would reassert itself at any time and she wanted to be well away by then.

They escaped easily and were soon driving along the road with nothing but the sunlight and the trees, the sound of the sea and the sweet call of the birds to keep them company. It was safe, tranquil again and she felt very pleased that they had left the other two behind. She had no doubt that Louisa would betray them and that Christian would frighten out of her the fact that she had packed two lunches. Stephanie grinned to herself. She had told Louisa that they intended to go to the beach across the island. If Christian pursued them there it would be a wild-goose chase.

She parked in the shade of the trees as the road finally petered out and together she and Jean-Paul climbed down to the cove and stood looking at the sea.

'Smugglers came here long ago,' Jean-Paul informed her, adding proudly, 'They were French smugglers and pirates.'

Stephanie nodded. She could well believe it. Her mind rapidly clothed Christian Durand in the costume of long ago and she was a little alarmed to find that the outfit suited him admirably. With his dark hair, tanned skin and brilliant eyes he could easily have been a pirate and she gave the idea up rapidly as her imagination had him swinging aboard some sailing ship, his superb muscles outlined against a silken shirt. At this rate she would terrify herself!

'Let's swim,' she ordered briskly and as Jean-Paul had been waiting for that command she had no further trouble. She closed her imagination down tightly and hammered on the lid.

It was a beautiful day. They swam, gathered shells and waded in the rock-pools. Jean-Paul was a delightful companion and except for an uneasy fluttering at the very back of her mind Stephanie never thought of Christian at all. It was only as they saw the sun begin to lose power and had to make the climb back to the Jeep that she let him come into her head. When he did, she immediately stiffened, preparing for combat because she knew and had known all the time that she would not easily get away with this outright insubordination.

'Is everything all right?' Jean-Paul enquired, picking up her mood. Stephanie nodded thoughtfully and threw a bright smile in his direction.

'Of course! What could be wrong on such a great day?'

'Why, nothing at all,' he laughed. 'Wait until Oncle Christian hears about our great day.'

Stephanie nodded again and managed another smile. Yes. Just wait until he heard about it! She took a deep breath and prepared her mind. There would be trouble and it would be about six feet two, lean-hipped, broad-shouldered and raging. It would try to destroy her with blue laser beams. She almost closed her eyes in anticipation and she had to admit that she would have preferred an actual physical fight, especially if she was given the opportunity to throw heavy things from a distance.

They arrived home a good deal earlier than they had on the previous night and Stephanie hated to think that it was because she had been anxious to avoid trouble. In any case, trouble was already there waiting and it pounced on her immediately.

'Go to your room at once, if you please, Jean-Paul,' Christian ordered as they walked into the house. This time he had not bothered to come and meet them. He knew he could get them with no effort at all and he never even looked at Stephanie.

'But, Oncle Christian, I want to tell you about our great day!' Jean-Paul protested but there was not one ounce of compromise on Christian's face.

'I will hear later, when you are in bed,' he said firmly. 'Tonight you shall have a tray in your room as you look tired. Meanwhile, your aunt Stephanie will explain to me the wider details of your day.'

Jean-Paul gave a very Gallic shrug and looked at Stephanie sympathetically. He knew that Christian was angry in spite of the quiet words. He made his get-away while he could and Stephanie turned to face the music.

Denise was there in a short cocktail dress, her eyes very interested and scornful. Once again, Stephanie was in shorts but this time she had taken certain precautions. The outfit was one of her new ones, a brilliant cotton with glowing colours. The shorts and halter-top had a matching skirt that buttoned from the knee up and she felt she could stand any type of scathing appraisal.

She was quite wrong. Christian waited until Jean-Paul was out of sight and then he looked her over with such annoyance and distaste that her cheeks flushed like a guilty schoolgirl. It was not the sort of look he had given her this morning as he had stood outside her room. She could have dealt with that, now that she had her mind under control. This look was contemptuous.

He turned away from her and gave his attention to Denise.

'I must speak to Mademoiselle Caine in private,' he said quietly. 'I'm sure you understand, Denise?'

'But of course! I have to prepare for dinner in any case.' She left with a pleased smile, knowing perfectly well that Christian was simply keeping a raging temper under temporary control. Denise was delighted with this turn of events and Stephanie assumed that Christian had been discussing her own shortcomings with the woman as he waited for them to return from the trip.

'Where have you been?' he asked in a softly menacing voice and his quiet words alarmed her more than any violence.

'Out for the day. We took a packed lunch.' She tried for nonchalance and almost succeeded.

'And left a few false clues behind you,' he finished acidly. 'You were going to the beach at the other side of the island, according to your words to Louisa. You did not go there, *mademoiselle*.'

'It's a huge beach. How can you possibly know that?' Stephanie asked scathingly and his answer really shocked her.

'I know because I have had the entire beach searched. We could not find you, neither could the police.'

'The police?' She just stared at him in amazement. 'Do you mean to tell me you're so intent on having your orders obeyed that you turned out the police to find us?'

'To find Jean-Paul, *mademoiselle*, not you. You may go where you will, disappear if the inclination takes you, but my nephew will not leave this house from this moment on. He will be allowed in the garden and he will go no further.'

'*I* am in charge of Jean-Paul!' Stephanie raged. 'I'll take him wherever I think fit.'

'I doubt if you are even in charge of yourself,' Christian rasped, pinning her with blue-eyed distaste. 'There is not one atom of responsibility in you. Your time as Jean-Paul's companion is over, *mademoiselle*. From now on, he stays with me!'

So far their voices had been low although the tone was acid enough to melt metal. Now, however, Stephanie forgot to keep her voice down. She was seething with rage and she quite forgot that Jean-Paul would be able to hear any raised voices. She raised hers.

'Listen,' she shouted. 'There's no way that you're ordering me about. You may be the most important monster around here but you're not *my* monster!'

CHAPTER THREE

STEPHANIE intended to expand on that theme but shock silenced her as Christian stepped forward, swept her up into strong, hard arms and strode off with her to Thierry's study, slamming the door shut behind him with his foot.

'Put me down!' she shouted again and this time she launched an attack on him with a great deal of vigour. The shock was wearing off and red-hot indignation was taking its place. She kicked out with her long legs and used her fists to land blows on his arms and back, only missing his face when he skilfully twisted his head out of the way. 'How dare you lay your—your vile French hands on me? Put me down!'

He dumped her unceremoniously on the leather settee and towered over her, his physical presence just daring her to move.

'You wish the whole island to hear us? You will sit there and listen to me,' he grated, glaring at her. Her skirt had come unfastened in the turmoil and now it was simply attached at the waist but there was a look about him that made her sit as still as a mouse and she never attempted to move at all.

'I have tried to keep you out of this,' he pointed out furiously. 'I have tried to take control quietly and allow you either to leave or simply enjoy a holiday but you have behaved with complete irresponsibility. *Tiens*! With you here the whole scene has changed and I now have two responsibilities instead of one!'

'I'm not...' Stephanie began angrily, but she got no further.

41

'Since nothing seems to penetrate your mind we will have to try fear, *mademoiselle*,' he snapped. 'My rules are not the rules of a tyrant, as you seem to think. As a very busy monster I have other things to do with my time. I came here in great haste to see Fiona, not realising that she had gone off with Thierry, showing the same lack of responsibility that you show yourself. Obviously it is inherited and I must see to it that my nephew is educated out of that particular English trait.'

Stephanie reddened with annoyance. That remark was because she had mentioned his vile French hands and it was obvious that he intended to change Jean-Paul. Fiona had been quite right. This was war! As to fear, she didn't admit to it and the sooner he learned that the better.

'You have no right to interfere with anything,' she informed him angrily. 'Fiona is entitled to a holiday and everything was just fine until you appeared on the scene with your power-crazed notions and . . . !'

'Are you ever silent, *mademoiselle*?' he asked furiously, still towering over her. 'I wonder if the truth will still your tongue? I am not here to interfere with anything. I would not care to intrude into your peculiar life. Do as you please, rage, scream and leave tomorrow. You mean nothing to me at all. I am here because of Jean-Paul.'

'To give him a hard time,' Stephanie concluded heatedly, looking up at him with blazing eyes. 'You're here to make him suitably submissive before you cart him off to France and take over his life!'

He stood quite still and stared at her, his dark brows drawn together.

'This is what you believe? Jean-Paul is my nephew. I have as much affection for him as you have, probably more. I am here to protect him.'

'You've got a strange way of going about it,' Stephanie told him scathingly. 'What do you intend to do, protect him from enjoying himself?'

'If necessary.' He went on looking at her, clearly torn between ordering her to her room and explaining his attitude further. 'I am very wealthy, *mademoiselle*,' he said, obviously making his mind up with reluctance. 'I have two relatives only—my brother Thierry and my nephew Jean-Paul. Unless I am vigilant, unless we are all vigilant, before my brother returns Jean-Paul will have disappeared.'

'What do you mean—disappeared?' Stephanie sat up straight and looked at him, her senses finally alert to danger. More than anything else, his suddenly quiet tone and his decision to speak to her calmly penetrated her mind. She could see that he was serious.

Christian reached into his pocket and drew out a letter, handing it to her.

'He will be kidnapped,' he assured her in the same quiet, even voice.

For a moment she stared at him in horror and then she looked at the letter, opening it and reading the few words there. Its brevity was sinister. It merely gave a name and an address.

Jean-Paul Durand.
The island of St Lucien.

Stephanie read the few words several times, not quite able to take it in. This was completely outside her world, something she could hardly believe, but it was real enough and if she had been inclined to dismiss it Christian's expression would have silenced her. It was deadly serious to him. People from his world could easily comprehend threats for money.

'We've got to get Fiona and Thierry back here at once,' she told him urgently but he glanced at her impatiently and turned away.

'You imagine I have not thought of that?' he grated. 'Do *you* know where they are?' When she shook her head he glared at her. 'So much for the trust your sister placed in you, *mademoiselle*. She does not even let you know her destination. I have people searching for them but as yet I have no idea where they are. My brother is supposed to be in Canada but not until next week. I foolishly believed that they would be here when I arrived but it is apparent that they have planned some second honeymoon and have decided simply to vanish.'

Now was not the time to tell him exactly why Fiona had decided that they should vanish and Stephanie looked at him worriedly. What had seemed like a brilliant idea now seemed extremely foolish.

'But why didn't you contact them before you left Paris?' she asked. 'You could have phoned and stopped all this.'

'A telephone call will not stop desperate people who are intent on kidnapping,' he snapped. 'As to phoning your sister and Thierry, I was already in Martinique when I received the note. I came at once, hoping to lessen the blow by being here myself. I found you here instead and your behaviour has not impressed me at all. I can only be thankful that I arrived speedily.'

'How was I to know anything about this?' Stephanie asked angrily. 'I would have behaved quite differently had I known that Jean-Paul was in danger. You never even told me yesterday and I had every right to know. It was because of you and your attitude that I went off today with Jean-Paul. Without realising it I put him in danger.'

'And yourself too, *mademoiselle*,' he rasped. 'I do not think they would have taken Jean-Paul with a polite murmur of regret and with your ability to fight back and infuriate I suspect they would have dealt with you very firmly indeed.'

Stephanie thought of the lonely, deserted cove. They hadn't seen a soul all day and if there had been any danger there would have been no help at all. She had deliberately left false clues behind and it had worked frighteningly well. An attack could have occurred at any time of the day. For all she knew, villains could have been following them and they were probably watching the house right now.

'Let's get him out of here,' she said quickly. 'Let's just pack his things and go!'

'I am pleased to find you including me in your plans,' Christian assured her scathingly. 'However, they are, as usual, unsound plans. On this island we can contain things. Strangers are noted and we have the best position. It would be difficult to take us by surprise here. *You* may go, of course, and it would be wise.'

'How dare you be so insulting?' Stephanie raged, jumping up. 'Do you imagine I'd run for cover, go back to London and get on with my life, leaving Jean-Paul in danger?'

Christian looked at her with a great deal of irritation.

'As far as you are concerned I keep my imagination tightly controlled,' he informed her. 'No insult was intended. I merely thought it would be better to have one less person to guard.'

'I'm perfectly capable of guarding myself as well as Jean-Paul,' Stephanie informed him tartly. 'Or do you expect a mass attack?'

'I do not know what to expect.' He turned away, pacing about, his hands in his pockets, and Stephanie slowly sat down again. It seemed like madness to her just to wait for events to take place but Christian seemed to have the upper hand now and she admitted that he was probably better equipped to deal with this sort of thing than she was herself. He probably knew a lot more than he was telling her too. He refused to acknowledge that she was deeply involved. Still, she had her own secrets. If Christian knew what she and Fiona had planned and why they had planned it, he would be furious, more furious than he was now.

'If we're staying here to see it out, we'll have to draw up some sort of plan,' she mused quietly, her mind running over the best positions for defence. If Christian wouldn't plan she had to do it herself. 'We could...'

'You will either leave St Lucien right now or do exactly as you are told!' Christian swung round, interrupting her with swift severity. 'I do not expect women to cope with this type of thing and I certainly do not intend to let *you* plan anything at all!'

'Ah!' Stephanie looked up at him angrily, her quiet musing ended. It seemed that chauvinism was rearing its head and she wasn't a bit surprised. 'That's a very strange remark,' she pointed out sharply. 'I distinctly remember you informing me that Madame Pascal was here to help take care of Jean-Paul. Does she have special qualifications? She doesn't look much like a black-belt karate expert to me.'

'Denise is older,' he reminded her acidly. 'She is more experienced.'

'I can believe it!' Stephanie snapped and he scowled at her darkly but she went on regardless. 'Being younger, though, I'm probably faster on my feet. I could have Jean-Paul away while Madame Pascal was putting the finishing touches to her face.'

Christian raised one black brow and stared at her, his eyes raking over her disparagingly.

'You are certainly younger,' he agreed drily. 'At the moment you are all long, slender legs and large, angry eyes. A little of Denise's sophistication would do you no harm at all. Obviously it will be necessary to speak further about the problem we have but for now, Mademoiselle Caine, I suggest you have a quiet, soothing word with your nephew before dinner. I would think that he heard your angry shouting. It was probably heard on the beach, perhaps even out to sea.'

Stephanie found to her extreme annoyance that his words were making her cheeks glow hotly; so was the scathing look. He was good at that. He had made her feel rather desperate this morning as he'd stood outside the bedroom door. And she knew he was right in any case because she had quite forgotten that her cleverly concealing skirt was now no concealment at all. Jean-Paul had quite likely been worried at hearing her shout too.

She pulled her skirt around her and stood but she couldn't bring herself simply to march out. She was not by any means finished with this discussion.

'Where's your car?' she asked unexpectedly, changing her tack with skill.

It astonished him and she could see his mind assessing her mental problems worriedly.

'I came by launch,' he informed her carefully, a puzzled look on his face. 'And before you remark that it is a long way from France, I will also let you into the secret that I brought my yacht with me. It is anchored around the headland.'

'Why?' Stephanie was instantly intrigued and her face showed it. He must have a plan after all and she was determined to know what it was. Whatever Christian did she was quite certain that Jean-Paul would be more comfortable with her than with anyone else. She was going to protect him herself and knowing as much as possible was necessary.

'It is a safe base. Also, as I had sailed to Martinique it seemed to be a very sound idea to bring the boat onwards to St Lucien. Should it be necessary, we will go out to the boat and stay there.'

Her mind had him back in the pirate outfit again and Stephanie stared at him fixedly, plans running round in her mind. Why hadn't he taken Jean-Paul there at once?

It was the obvious solution. Nobody could just walk on to a boat unseen.

'Let's go out there now,' she urged vehemently. 'Why are we hanging around here? You want to contain things? What better place than a boat? Let's just pick Jean-Paul up and get out to the yacht. We could ward off an attack!'

'We are not about to be attacked.' Christian walked slowly forward and stopped, looking down at her frantic face. 'Somebody intends simply to take Jean-Paul away. It will be done with a certain finesse and I very much doubt if it will include a set of rogues armed with cutlasses.'

'What makes you so sure?' Stephanie wanted to know and he looked at her steadily, weighing his words, once again wondering how much to divulge.

'I am sure because it is their way,' he informed her quietly. 'Several leading industrialists have faced this problem and not all of them have escaped unscathed in the end. There is a lot of money involved. It is a very simple business transaction. You remove a loved one and demand payment.'

'Then why don't they just kidnap you? You're the big fish.'

'I would be more difficult to handle than a small boy. All they want is the money.'

'Pay them!' Stephanie ordered vehemently. 'You must be rolling in hard cash. Just pay up!'

'Sometimes they cheat,' he said coolly. 'The last time, a young girl was not returned. I intend to catch them and I do not intend to place Jean-Paul in jeopardy. If they fail and are not caught, they will try again. There is, in fact, nothing to stop them trying regularly. I cannot have Jean-Paul constantly exposed to danger.'

'You can't avoid it,' Stephanie surmised worriedly, biting at her lip as his words sank in.

'I can. I will deal with it, believe me. All I ask is that you obey me at all times. Leave me to do the thinking.'

'I can think!'

'When you think less impetuously we will join forces. *Alors*! It is almost time for dinner. Dare I suggest a change of costume, *mademoiselle*?'

This time, Stephanie never thought of arguing with him. She went off very thoughtfully and was thankful to see Jean-Paul safely in his room, sitting up in bed, eating his supper.

'Pampered child,' she joked, wanting to hug him tightly and sit by the bed on permanent guard. 'Nobody offered to feed me in bed.'

'I expect I am Oncle Christian's pet,' he grinned. 'He was quite right too, I am tired. If I get to sleep early we can perhaps go on another expedition tomorrow, Stevie?'

'We'll have to wait and see.' She smiled and went to her own room. The expeditions were over. From now on all she could do was follow her nephew around and watch him at all times. She only hoped they could keep this worry away from him. If only Thierry and Fiona would come back. If only she had insisted on knowing where they were going. It would be better to have plenty of people guarding Jean-Paul and who better than his own mother and father?

A cynical, handsome face came into her mind and she grimaced. Christian was better. He was tough, clever and had a look of ruthlessness about him that Thierry would never have. He also commanded millions, if Fiona's words were to be believed. Any help he needed he could call up without delay. The trouble was that he didn't seem to have called any help at all, except for getting the police to search for her this afternoon. She could almost be sure he hadn't told them anything. He wouldn't have told *her* unless he had been forced to.

As she showered the sand away from her skin and hair, Stephanie went on thinking about the problem. Christian seemed to be in no doubt that the note was serious. He had known it to happen before and had the look about him of someone who was preparing for a battle. As far as she could see, though, they were sitting ducks. One careless moment and Jean-Paul could be taken.

She had never thought that wealth could bring such worries. Her life had been quite carefree so far but she could see now that someone like Christian Durand would have to be hard in many ways. She could understand why he no longer had that indulgent look about him that she had imagined when she was nineteen. The years would have added to his responsibilities.

When she walked back into her room she caught sight of herself in the mirror and nodded ruefully. He was quite right. She looked tousled and too young, not one bit of sophistication about her. If she continued to look like this then Christian was never going to allow her to have any part in guarding Jean-Paul. It was time to be the Celestial Girl again.

She frowned at herself. Christian Durand was certainly ready with his insults. He had pointedly remarked about her appearance. He talked like that because he felt superior and older, as if he were *her* uncle Christian too. It was time to bring him to heel and she got out her make-up box determinedly.

Even so, as she went down to dinner, Stephanie was more anxious than defiant. She had this terrible feeling that something would happen at once, that they had taken no precautions whatever and that the house was being watched. She walked into the drawing-room with a thoughtful look on her face and she was so accustomed to being well groomed and dressed for an occasion that she had quite forgotten that there was anything unusual about her appearance.

She had done her hair as the advertisement required, swept up and swirled around her face. The silver-gilt strands glittered in the lamplight and her make-up was perfect, years of practice making it look utterly natural. She hadn't brought many things for the evening because she had not intended to be involved in any kind of formality but there were the silk skirts and tops she had brought back from the Canaries and she wore one of those outfits now. It was dark red and her silver bracelets matched her silver shoes.

The look on Christian's face stopped her in her tracks and quite embarrassed her out of thoughtfulness. He stood with his drink and just stared at her with those brilliant eyes until she began to think she had made some sort of terrible mistake. As far as she could think, she had not. Her skirt was fastened and fitted silkily to her hips, her top was a camisole and she had definitely put it on.

She found herself blushing once again and the sophistication was most certainly teetering on the edge. It was ridiculous! She had never been bothered about people looking at her. If she had been, she would have been out of business years ago.

Christian bothered her, though, and he didn't seem to care that he was embarrassing her. His eyes were moving over her as if he was intent on photographing her image on his mind. He was inspecting every inch of her figure with a concentration that left her feeling breathless. Nobody had aroused such strong feelings in her before and she didn't exactly know what to do. Her legs were shaky and his eyes narrowed thoughtfully as if he knew how she was feeling.

Denise Pascal looked from one to the other angrily but Christian never seemed to notice.

'I've seen you before!' Denise suddenly pounced as if she was determined to break the odd spell that had come over Christian.

'I'm pleased you remember,' Stephanie murmured, avoiding Christian's eyes. 'I'm staying here. We had dinner together last night if you recall.'

'I mean somewhere else.' Denise moved her hand impatiently and looked at Stephanie with hard, suspicious eyes. 'It is probably a trick of the light but you remind me of something.'

'I think the trick was played yesterday and earlier today,' Christian surmised softly. 'We are seeing the real Mademoiselle Caine at last, are we not?'

'I'm the same person who went upstairs not long ago,' Stephanie managed, just glancing at him and then looking away quickly. She hardly dared to move. It was like being bathed in brilliant light.

'*Au contraire*. You have aged remarkably.'

Stephanie didn't need to reply to this taunt because Denise had obviously had enough of the conversation. She tucked her arm possessively into Christian's and announced that she was ready to eat. It was a great relief to be able to move and not have to face such intent appraisal but once they were at the dinner-table Stephanie was furious to find that Louisa had made a muddle of the seating arrangements. It seemed that with the absence of Jean-Paul her ability to space things out had deserted her. She had placed Stephanie facing Christian. Of course, she might have intended that Denise should sit there but Denise moved close to Christian and sat next to him with a look on her face that told Stephanie that this was her normal, rightful place.

It wasn't surprising. He would not have brought this woman here if she hadn't been with him on the yacht and she would not have been there if she had not been his mistress. Stephanie looked at him with a great deal of scorn—at least, she intended to but he was still watching her, his eyes now slightly closed but still moving over her appraisingly. She felt the need to look away fast, almost to duck her head. She was not going to put up with this for much longer. He intended to belittle her and nobody had managed that in her whole life.

She ate her meal in silence, hardly taking any notice of the other two. Denise spoke softly and intimately to Christian, keeping Stephanie out of their little world but she didn't want to be in it anyway. There was safety in silence. She wasn't sure if she would be able to hold her own with Christian at the moment. She was still aware of the danger that surrounded them too and she wanted to get back upstairs to Jean-Paul.

Finally she felt the need to take action and she interrupted their conversation with the urgency that she was feeling in her voice.

'What are we going to do?' she demanded, looking determinedly at Christian. 'There's the whole night to get through and we haven't planned anything. We can't just leave things as they are. It's too serious for that.'

'What is so serious?' Denise turned furious green eyes on Stephanie, her tongue obviously ready to drip poison, but Christian intervened smoothly before any harsh words could be said.

'It is nothing, *ma chère*,' he soothed, taking Denise by the hand. 'I will deal with your worries tomorrow, Stephanie,' he added, looking at her with annoyed eyes. 'Don't be so anxious about your sister. I'm sure they intended to disappear for a second honeymoon. It doesn't matter. Jean-Paul has plenty of company and next week Thierry will definitely be in Canada.'

Stephanie stared at him in surprise and then it dawned on her. Denise Pascal knew nothing at all about the danger. It told her several things, one of them being that the woman was not here to take care of Jean-Paul in any way. She was just with Christian. In the middle of something terrible, he had brought his mistress along. It disgusted her and her feelings showed on her face.

He had also used a very patronising tone—called her Stephanie and spoken to her as if she were an idiot. She ate the rest of her meal in silence, determined to get him later. If Denise Pascal knew nothing then she was not about to enlighten her.

'Celestial!' Denise suddenly said triumphantly a few seconds later. 'I remember! I knew I had seen that face before. You are the girl that Celeste use for their products.'

'That's right.' Stephanie glanced up at her and then got on with her meal.

'But you are a model!' Denise made this pronouncement with a faint air of distaste but Stephanie could not be bothered with a battle at the moment. She had other things on her mind.

'It pays well.' She shrugged her slender shoulders and said nothing, keeping her caustic thoughts to herself. How working for a living could compare badly with being somebody's mistress quite escaped her but she was not at all interested in Denise Pascal's opinions. Her mind was working furiously in other directions. Christian was back to watching her intently and she rather thought he was willing her to behave herself. He could relax. She wanted action, not words.

Stephanie cornered him later, though. Denise went off to bed early, no doubt to wait for Christian, and when he went on to the veranda Stephanie put down the magazine she had been reading in between frequent trips to peep in at Jean-Paul. She had herself under control now. His intent looks were not going to bother her. Realising that he had brought his mistress here in the middle of all the danger had brought her rapidly to her senses.

'She doesn't know anything about this, does she?' Stephanie walked out to stand just under the lights and Christian glanced across at her, a flashing glance that moved over her beautiful face and slender figure.

'I thought it best not to alarm her.'

'You've put her in exactly the same position you placed me in,' Stephanie pointed out quietly. 'If she doesn't know about it she won't be able to take any precautions. You can hardly say you're keeping quiet because you don't trust her.'

'If it becomes necessary I will inform her. In the meantime, this is strictly between you and me.' He stared at her, holding her gaze with his. 'I do not want her upset. In any case, how do you know I trust her? She is a woman.'

'*Your* woman,' Stephanie corrected scathingly. 'So important to you that you brought her along in the middle of all this turmoil.'

He looked at her with narrowed eyes, obviously on the verge of losing his considerable temper.

'People normally keep out of my affairs,' he informed her acidly.

'Circumstances alter cases. I'm in this affair up to my neck and it seems to me that just the two of us are not even capable of guarding Jean-Paul. Now we have the added complication of Madame Pascal. What do I do if anything happens, fling myself in front of her protectively and advise Jean-Paul to run?'

'In a few days this will all be over,' he said stiffly, frowning at her with a good deal of concentration. 'I am not simply sitting here waiting as you seem to imagine. I have people following leads. Any stranger would be extremely lucky to get on to the island.'

'You could have told me!' Stephanie snapped and he shrugged and turned away.

'I did not choose to. You are only on the edge of this affair, involved by accident. The only reason you know anything at all is because you cannot be trusted to act in a reasonable manner. I rather suspect that your more mature looks will not alter your basic instinct to behave irrationally. You now look like a woman but I very much doubt if you will behave like one.'

'As you're obviously knowledgeable about women you'll be able to judge!' Stephanie seethed. 'As to this being over soon, time will tell. No doubt you'll be going very speedily then. I long for the day.'

'We are in agreement at last,' he remarked bitingly. 'Perhaps in the meantime you could try not to disrupt my life too much?'

'What do you mean?' Stephanie immediately prepared to battle but his next words rather took the wind out of her sails. He turned to look at her, leaning back against the veranda rail.

'You insisted, rather desperately, on planning our night, *mademoiselle*. I had to do some fast thinking.'

'You knew perfectly well what I meant!' Stephanie snapped, her cheeks flushing brightly.

'Denise did not.'

'I'm surprised,' Stephanie retorted. 'Knowing how she's going to pass the night, I can't imagine her being interested in my problems.'

He just stood and laughed at her, evidently enjoying this, his annoyance gone now that he had her embarrassed, and Stephanie swung round to march off.

'Goodnight, Stephanie,' he said with dark, malicious amusement in his voice and she turned on him furiously.

'Goodnight,' she snapped. 'And *mademoiselle* will do quite well, thank you!'

It was all right to be in a rage but it didn't last long. Embarrassment seemed unimportant at the side of the big problem. Stephanie got ready for bed and then sat in the dark for ages, peering out of the window, thankful that this was a two-storey house. It would be a bit more difficult to get in here than if they had just been able to gain entrance from the veranda and in spite of Christian's words she was still certain that they were close to the house.

She didn't even know who 'they' were. Christian had told her very little, just as much as she needed to know and nothing more. She could well understand that he was accustomed to keeping his own counsel and making his own decisions but this was a little different from the business world. This was the criminal world and Jean-Paul's safety was at stake. She was involved whether he liked it or not.

A slight noise had her looking round, instantly alert, and as she listened she was sure it was someone on the passage outside. She ran to the door on her bare feet and peered out but the softly lit passage was empty and she was certain then that it must be somebody in Jean-Paul's room. He was next to her and she would have heard exactly the sounds she had heard if somebody had crept in there.

She had no idea where Christian was sleeping or she would have raced along to get him and risked upsetting Denise but in any case there might not be time. Tackling them now was essential. There was nothing to take with her for a weapon either. She looked frantically round her room but nothing seemed to be heavy enough or sharp enough. Her hairdrier was the only thing. Aimed at the right place it could do some damage and she would then be able to shout for Christian.

Stephanie crept out on to the passage and approached Jean-Paul's door and her heart began to hammer alarmingly when it slowly opened before she could even get her hand on the handle. She flattened herself against the outside wall, the hairdrier raised for action. Whoever came out was not getting past her.

Jean-Paul wasn't crying out either. They must have tied him up. She was so angry at the thought that she really felt pleased to be able to bring the drier down on some fiendish head. She brought it down with as much force as possible and gasped with shock when her wrist was grasped and twisted cruelly as Christian ducked his head smartly out of the way.

For a second he stared furiously into her frantic face and then he grasped her arm and almost pushed her back to her room. Her feet seemed to be leaving the floor but he said nothing at all until she was inside her own room and the door closed.

CHAPTER FOUR

'ARE you mad?' Christian snapped in a low voice, his grip tightening painfully. 'What the devil are you doing, creeping about like an assassin?'

'I heard a noise.' Stephanie was still a little too shocked to defend herself. It had all taken her by surprise and Christian looked explosive. Even in the moonlight she could see anger and exasperation on his face. Surely he realised she was only doing her job?

'And I'm lucky to be able to hear anything at all,' he reminded her with quiet fury. 'Had I not seen your shadow you would now be beating me further with your contraption, no doubt.'

'I've got to guard Jean-Paul,' she protested, and that was obviously the wrong thing to say. He jerked her forward and jabbed one long finger at her.

'*Taisez-vous*! You will guard nothing at all. Whatever you look like, you are utterly irresponsible. Your presence is a danger to my nephew. Tomorrow I will send you back to England.'

'You will not! You don't have the authority and I'm not leaving Jean-Paul. Suppose it had been one of the kidnappers in his room just now?'

'Then he would still be there, *mademoiselle*, much the worse for wear. *I* was in Jean-Paul's room and any intruder would have known it to his cost. There would have been nobody for you to beat senseless!'

'I didn't know that,' Stephanie protested. 'I can't see how you can be so annoyed when I was just doing my job.'

'It is not your job to knock me unconscious. Neither is it your job to creep about in the middle of the night. I know exactly what I am about and things will be much safer if you are in England and back in front of a camera where you can do no damage.'

'I'm not going,' Stephanie stated stubbornly. 'Don't even try it. I can be big trouble.'

'I have never doubted it for even a moment,' he snapped. 'You prove it constantly.'

It was ridiculous standing in the near-darkness, hissing furiously at each other, and Christian obviously thought so too. He muttered under his breath and let her go as he made an exasperated movement towards the light switch.

'Don't!' Stephanie's urgent warning stopped him and he looked at her closely.

'*Pourquoi?*'

'Somebody might be out there,' she whispered and he glared at her again, turning back to the switch.

'There is no need to prove insanity. I accept the fact readily!'

'And I'm not dressed,' she finished breathlessly, pleased when that stopped him completely.

'Then I suggest you get into bed,' he advised acidly. 'Tomorrow may well be your big day. You will either be fighting off invaders or being put on a plane for home. For either event you need sleep.'

He turned to the door but Stephanie still stood there.

'How can I sleep? Jean-Paul is lying there so innocently. He just doesn't know he's in danger.'

'And I do not intend for him to find out,' Christian warned her savagely. He suddenly relaxed and took a step back towards her. 'Go to sleep. *I* am guarding Jean-Paul. Nothing will happen to him during the night.'

'You'll be tired, then,' Stephanie muttered. 'You'll not be fit to tackle anything tomorrow.'

'You think not? I am surprised. Surely you know that the wicked never sleep? Go to bed, *mademoiselle*. We are both lucky after all. I am not unconscious and, as I did not have to grapple with you, you are safe.' His eyes probed hers in the near-darkness. 'A silky adversary may have been too much for my self-restraint. Perhaps you would have found a way to pass your night.'

He had gone before she could speak, not that she had any ready retort. She wasn't used to dealing with men like Christian Durand. He was far too masculine to be easily dismissed. In future she would have to watch her step. One thing had come out of it, though—he hadn't actually said he would send her home tomorrow, not at the last minute anyway. She wouldn't go in any case. It would take more than Christian to guard Jean-Paul and as far as she was concerned they were in this together, almost partners. Christian might as well get used to the idea.

Stephanie settled into bed, watching the moonlit window for a moment, but her eyes began to feel heavy and she knew she would be able to sleep after all. It was because Christian was awake. It made her feel safe and it made her feel that there was security for Jean-Paul.

A funny feeling unfurled at the pit of her stomach when she thought of Christian looking at her. It faded, though, when she remembered Denise Pascal. What was Denise making of these night-time excursions? She would be sleeping alone or sitting up fuming.

It served her right. The woman had no business being here. Anyway, she was married, or perhaps divorced? Whatever she was, she was by herself tonight. Christian really cared for his nephew—*their* nephew!

Stephanie gave a wicked little smile and fell asleep. The only way he could get rid of her was by using superior physical force and she had every intention of creating a scene if he tried it. Nobody was separating her from Jean-Paul. She would guard him every minute and when this was over the problem of his schooling could be dealt with. Thierry would come back a changed man. Fiona would see to that.

Next morning, Stephanie was very tired. She went down to breakfast looking pale and worried and was startled to find only Christian there.

'Where is Jean-Paul?' she asked immediately and Christian nodded towards the veranda.

'Out there. Don't worry, I can see him all the time.' He stood and pulled out a chair for her. 'He was intent on waking you but I told him you would probably be tired.' He sat facing her and let his gaze roam over her face. 'You look pale,' he pointed out softly. 'I regret that I had to tell you about the problem. It would have been better to remain in a rage and send you home at once.'

'I wouldn't have gone in any case,' Stephanie muttered. 'Have you contacted Fiona and Thierry yet?' He shook his head as she looked up at him.

'When they are found I will be informed.'

'It must be frightening to wield so much power,' she mused aloud. 'If I had so much money, I'd cash it all in and just go away quietly.'

'And leave hundreds out of a job?' He looked at her quizzically. 'I do not think you would. Anyhow, these things grow on you. Before you know it you are responsible for so much that it is impossible to step back.'

'I hadn't thought of that.' When she said nothing else he regarded her with cool amusement.

'You do not wish to argue the point, *mademoiselle*? I assume that you are too tired to battle as yet.'

'I won't battle,' she sighed. 'Just let me help. Admit that I'm in this. You'll only get a battle if you insist that I leave Jean-Paul.'

'Very well. We will join forces.' He said nothing more but it wasn't enough for Stephanie. She wanted action, preferably now.

'So tell me what you're going to do,' she insisted. 'I don't believe that you're going to do nothing. You must have a plan.'

'I intend to catch them. I have told you that.'

'You've told me as little as possible,' Stephanie pointed out. 'If we're to be partners I think I should know everything.'

'Partners? Knowing you, I assume you want equal status?'

'You don't know me,' she said flatly. 'I'll let the matter drop for now but just remember that I'm in this to the end.'

'It may be dangerous,' he reminded her. 'I cannot guarantee your safety.'

'I'm only interested in Jean-Paul's safety,' Stephanie said, glancing up at him. 'I can take care of myself. What I'm asking is that you let me know your plans.'

'You have just told me that I do not know you, *mademoiselle*,' he reminded her. 'And you are right. If I knew you better I might be inclined to take you into my confidence.'

Jean-Paul ran in then, coming to give Stephanie a morning kiss, and she had to let the matter drop. It seemed to her that Christian took nobody into his confidence. Denise Pascal was his mistress and yet he was quite content to let her be ignorant of the danger she was probably in right now.

'What shall we do today?' Jean-Paul stood beside her, looking at her eagerly, expecting instant action. 'Stevie is clever at arranging things,' he added for Christian's benefit.

'But not today,' Stephanie said quickly. 'I'm tired. I didn't get my supper in bed if you recall. Today we can just stay in the garden and maybe swim in the pool.'

'What about expeditions?' Jean-Paul asked indignantly but she stood up, leaving the meal she didn't really want and urging him back out into the sunshine.

'Expeditions are temporarily cancelled,' she announced. 'Everyone is confined to barracks.' She wanted to make quite sure that Christian knew she was keeping her side of the bargain and he gave her a twisted smile as she walked out. It was a very sardonic smile and she was quite aware that keeping her side of the bargain would not mean that he would keep his. He didn't trust her.

'Oncle Christian will call you Stevie before too long,' Jean-Paul remarked smugly as they stepped down on to the lawn. 'He is speaking to you a lot.'

'He's being polite,' Stephanie said quickly. 'When I've had a minute, I'll swim with you,' she promised, anxious to take his mind off Uncle Christian. She had enough to do with watching and waiting. Affectionate names from someone like Christian Durand was an alarming thought, not even to be contemplated. Just thinking about him unsettled her and she was quite sure that this truce between them would not last for very long. He would do something infuriating and she would go for him at once.

Jean-Paul soon became bored and told Stephanie so. It was obvious that keeping him around the house would be difficult without explaining to him just why it was necessary. He was an extremely intelligent little boy and it would not be long before he became suspicious.

They were sitting by the pool and Denise was sticking to Christian as closely as possible, her eyes suspiciously on Stephanie every time she tried to attract Christian's attention. It was impossible and when Denise went indoors for a minute Stephanie tackled him.

'Look,' she said firmly. 'We can't go on like this. Jean-Paul is bored out of his mind and this is just the first morning of the new rules. Much more of this with both of us watching him and he's going to be suspicious.'

'I know and I have noticed his boredom,' Christian assured her quietly.

'Well, what are we going to do? At least you could tell Madame Pascal and then we could talk openly.'

'I have no intention of telling Denise,' he snapped. 'She is not to be worried. I have already said that.'

He got up and walked to the edge of the long green lawn, standing to look down on the beach. It was deserted. This was not a private beach but few people came to this part of the island. The most that ever happened was that a few islanders would come to collect driftwood. Today there was nobody.

'Jean-Paul could perhaps go down on the beach for a while,' Christian continued, his eyes scanning the empty sands. 'We will all go.'

Stephanie made no attempt to argue. She was very uneasy. There was even danger in the silence of the beach and she looked out along the sand dunes and rocks, searching for likely hiding places. As far as she could see there was nobody at all but she was glad that Christian was coming, even if Denise had to come too.

'Relax.' When she stood there nibbling at her lip and worrying, Christian squeezed her shoulder in an unexpectedly comforting gesture. 'Very little can happen if we are all there.'

She wasn't too sure of that, having hordes of rogues in mind, but as it turned out, after one searching look at them, Denise declined the honour and just the three of them made the descent to the beach after lunch. Denise elected to sit by the pool and Stephanie was glad. With a woman like that there, any spare attention would have to be given to her and it would take all their efforts to guard Jean-Paul.

'Did you really intend Madame Pascal to help look after Jean-Paul?' she asked quietly as they walked along the sand together and Jean-Paul skipped ahead happily. 'I can't really see her in the role of child-minder.'

Christian never looked at her, he simply kept on walking and for a few seconds she thought he wasn't going to bother to answer.

'She was with me,' he finally acknowledged stiffly. 'Short of offering her a rowing boat and a compass there was little I could do about bringing her here. I had to come to St Lucien and that is what I did.'

'Didn't you think about the fact that you've probably put her in danger?' Stephanie persisted. 'She seems blissfully unaware of any undercurrents. When they pounce on her she'll be startled out of her mind.'

'Your concern is quite touching,' he murmured drily, slanting a sceptical look at her. 'They are not, however, going to pounce on her. As a matter of fact, I had planned to send her away when I sent you.'

'That wasn't what you said,' Stephanie pointed out triumphantly. 'She was going to look after Jean-Paul after I'd been dispatched. I'm beginning to wonder if you ever tell the truth.'

'It seemed a good way of getting rid of you. I would have changed my mind at the last minute and sent you off together. It was my intention,' he told her complacently.

Stephanie stopped and looked up at him, her eyes searching his face.

'You astound me,' she pronounced. 'You make these sweeping decisions as if this is a game of chess. You feel capable of taking on all comers single-handed?'

'I usually do.' His blue eyes met her puzzled gaze and she felt a burst of annoyance at his arrogance.

'"Usually" isn't exactly good enough when Jean-Paul's safety is at stake,' she reminded him as she turned away in irritation. 'It seems to me that the more the merrier is a better idea, although Madame Pascal is not exactly merry and we seem to be seeing less of her rather than more.'

'Nothing is about to happen yet,' he stated imperturbably and Stephanie gave him one of her better scowls.

'We'd damned well better hope so!' she snapped.

'Do you always speak like that?' he asked in a reprimanding tone and she didn't even bother to look at him.

'Only when driven by extreme exasperation.' She went on ahead, catching up with Jean-Paul, leaving Christian to do as he wished, and they went back to their favourite pastime, wading in the rock-pools and gathering shells.

If she stayed with Christian for much longer she was going to fly into a rage again. Nobody in her life had got under her skin so much. He was the most masculine being she had ever met and the most arrogant! He might have an odd effect on her from time to time but mostly his imperious ways just infuriated her.

As she glanced up later she could see him sitting on one of the higher rocks. He wasn't watching them but he looked irritatingly like a guard, a very relaxed one. He was so sure of himself that he wasn't even keeping a keen look-out. She could only hope that if anyone came they would grab him first and give her time to get Jean-Paul clear.

After a while, Jean-Paul went to the rocks and climbed up to sit next to Christian and Stephanie had to do the same unless she wanted to stay there alone and appear to be very churlish. In any case, she had no intention of missing out on anything. Whatever Christian said, *she* felt responsible for her nephew's safety and she wanted to make sure he did not get too close to Jean-Paul. There was still the little matter of school and his take-over bid.

She walked up and flung herself on the sand. If she was sunbathing it was a good excuse to keep her eyes closed. That way she didn't need to speak to him. It was bad enough that he had to be there. If that idiotic woman had come with them, she could have kept him occupied.

What was she here for after all but to amuse Christian Durand? Stephanie kept her eyes closed, scowled and tightened her lips.

'Do you get a lot of work?' Christian's sudden question had Stephanie looking up in surprise and she found that his eyes were skimming over her figure. Her tan had deepened, the sunlight on her hair picked out all the silvery lights and now a slowly gathering blush was making her more colourful than ever.

'She is in all the magazines and on the front of most of them,' Jean-Paul announced proudly while she was still sitting in stunned silence. 'Maman says that Stevie is the face of the year. She says that people try to copy Stevie's looks. Papa thinks she is perfect.'

He leapt down and began to throw stones at the sea, advancing a little way down the beach. It brought Stephanie to attention and she sat up quickly to keep an eye on him, although she could have done without the loyal little speech. It also gave her the opportunity to look away from Christian.

'You seem to have a devoted fan there,' he murmured drily. 'I would have thought him too young to really appreciate you. It must be because he is French.' He was still watching her, his gaze on her shining hair and the long brown legs that glistened silkily in the sunlight.

'I'm his friend,' Stephanie said sharply, irritated when she felt her cheeks begin to get hotter. She sat up quickly, drawing her legs under her for a bit of security from his brilliant scrutiny. 'In any case, I never talk about my job. Perhaps we could change the subject.'

'The subject is difficult to change. You seem to be constantly in my sight—usually uncovered.'

'I'm on holiday on a sunny island!' Stephanie snapped. 'I forgot to bring a sack with me but I'm sure I could make one given the necessary material!' She glared up at him and found to her annoyance that he was smiling down at her in a very sardonic manner, thoroughly enjoying her embarrassment.

'Please don't,' he begged wryly. 'It would be such a waste. I could watch you all day. You are astonishingly beautiful and I also find you most entertaining.'

He made Stephanie feel like a performing seal and she rounded on him swiftly. He was doing this deliberately to make her uneasy. He could save his expertise. She knew exactly what he was.

'Unlike your mistress, I work for a living,' she said coldly. 'It would be nice if you remembered that you're Jean-Paul's uncle and not mine!'

'I do not feel at all like your uncle, *mademoiselle*. If I feel anything at all about you, it is perhaps the anxiety of a keeper with an unruly charge in his custody.'

Stephanie's lips parted but she was momentarily speechless. She had never encountered such colossal impertinence. Before she could rage at him further, though, Louisa shouted from the bottom of the steps.

'Telephone, Monsieur Durand!' and Christian leapt down from the rocks, his sardonic attitude disappearing.

'It may be Thierry,' he stated grimly. 'I certainly hope it is.' He reached down quite automatically and pulled Stephanie to her feet, his eyes going swiftly to Jean-Paul. 'While it is probably quite safe here at the moment, I would be happier in my mind if you were to collect Jean-Paul and come back to the garden.'

Stephanie just nodded. She was quite ready to obey at a time like this. She was not about to let any battle with Christian endanger her nephew.

'I'll call him now,' she agreed and Christian walked off to the house, his manner utterly different from a few minutes ago.

Stephanie looked after him frustratedly. He was quite impossible and very clearly filled with a great deal of self-importance. The sooner this affair was resolved the better, because she would have to do something drastic if she stayed close to Christian Durand for very much longer. He had annoyed her right from the first. Now he was doing it deliberately and using masculine tricks to get the better of her.

She called Jean-Paul, cramming her straw hat on her head and walking down the beach towards him, preparing to go back to the house at once. With Christian's departure the air of menace seemed to have come back again and she was anxious to get on to higher ground where she could see anyone approaching.

It was quiet and still, with only the sound of the sea and the sigh of the soft wind that bent the palms; even so, there was the feeling that she should stay alert at all times. She couldn't shake off the sensation of being watched and now that Christian had gone the steps to the cliff seemed to be a long way off. From down here it was not even possible to see the house.

'Let's go!' she ordered urgently and Jean-Paul looked at her in surprise.

'Of course, Stevie. I want to just dabble my feet first, though. I am covered with sand.'

'You can do it at the house...' she began but he was already running to the sea and he never heard her. It put her in a dilemma. If she shouted and made a fuss he would be alarmed. He was not stupid and he would quickly see that she was anxious. She didn't want him frightened any more than Christian did. It was a question of weighing the odds.

She went down to join him, hoping to hurry him up by jollying him along. Down by the sea, she could see the house but it looked alarmingly distant. She chased Jean-Paul out of the water, hoping that her laughter did not sound forced because all the time she had her eyes on the sand dunes and the rocks.

'It was a waste of time,' Jean-Paul declared. 'I am just as sandy as ever. It was fun, though, yes?'

'Definitely,' Stephanie assured him, urging him forward at some speed. It seemed like ages since Christian had gone to the house but in actual fact she knew it was only minutes. It was irksome to discover just how much she relied on that irritating Frenchman now that there was danger and although she had spoken out strongly in her own favour on several occasions she knew she would need Christian if anything happened.

It was at that moment that she saw a slight movement behind the sand dunes and her heart took off at an alarming rate. She stared fixedly at the spot, telling herself that it was probably her own overwrought imagination or that it was some islander coming along the beach.

A second glimpse told her it was not. There were two men and they were white. Moreover, they were hiding, not in any obvious way or she would not have seen them but they were moving cautiously and carefully keeping to cover. If she hadn't been so alert she would not have spotted them at all.

The inclination was to run at once but a quick assessment told her that the men were in actual fact closer to the beach steps than she was. She would have to run with Jean-Paul across open sand and they would be cut off long before they reached safety. She could scream for Christian but there was no guarantee that he would hear her. He might still be on the telephone.

A diversion was needed and she thought quickly before saying brightly to Jean-Paul, 'I'll race you to the steps and into the house. I'll even give you a head start.'

'You are on.' He cunningly set off at once and it was just what she wanted. As Jean-Paul raced to the steps, Stephanie raced to the rocks. It was a straight line for her, not the diagonal track that Jean-Paul had to take, and the men would have to pass her before they could reach him. She couldn't see them now and it made her run even faster. If she could get to the rocks before they did she would have to stop them somehow.

Jean-Paul was almost halfway to the steps as she made it to her goal and he was so set on winning that he never looked round. She knew she had done the right thing because she could now hear low voices. They were speaking in French and she had no idea what they were saying but as Jean-Paul's name was mentioned she knew she had summed things up correctly. They were here to get him, just as she had feared. Her instincts had not betrayed her.

This was it, then and she had nobody to help at all. At any moment she would be facing the men who intended harm to her nephew; Stephanie's face tightened with determination. It was a 'them' and 'us' situation and she was not going to lose.

When they came carefully round the rocks she crouched down and as they drew level, she scooped up a hat full of sand and threw it straight into their faces, then ran as fast as she could. She expected to be caught but at least they would not get Jean-Paul. He was already at the top of the steps and as she looked Christian came to the edge of the grass and looked down at her.

'They're here!' she screamed, falling and getting up to run even faster. She saw him begin to come to her and she yelled at him, waving her arms. 'Go back! They'll kill you!'

He just ignored her warning and came on, reaching her in seconds and stopping her mad run for safety.

'Run!' she gasped but Christian simply held her fast by her shoulders, his eyes looking back the way she had come and instead on moving and helping her to safety, he then looked down at her with raised dark brows and an expression of utter incredulity on his face.

When she turned her head fearfully she could see the men almost staggering. Her aim, it seemed, had been excellent because neither of them could see. The sand had caught them full in the face and by the look of it most of the grains were in their eyes.

'I got them,' she panted triumphantly. 'I got them. Quick! Let's get back to the house.'

'Not before I help them,' Christian said bleakly. He had that look on his face again, as if she had done something stupid, and she stared at him wildly.

'Help them? They'll kill you! Are you mad?'

'To the best of my knowledge, no,' he assured her coolly. 'I am, however, beginning to have some very grave doubts about you.'

'What's mad about saving Jean-Paul from kidnappers?' she shouted, wriggling to get away from him and looking anxiously behind her.

'Nothing at all. It so happens, though, that the two men you have so obviously maimed are *my* men. Clearly they need help because for some reason they are staggering about. I assume that you have attempted to blind them.'

It stopped her struggles and Stephanie looked up at him blankly.

'Your men?'

'*Oui.* I have had two men stationed out here since I arrived. I had thought it better to be safe than sorry but I had not reckoned with English madness. Now I am merely sorry and of course I shall have to tell them so before I see what damage you have done.'

Stephanie wrenched herself away from him and looked up into two eyes that seemed on the edge of anger. She was trembling from her fright and from the wild run and now he was making her feel like an utter fool. She had even been worried that they would kill him. She had been forced to use courage she hadn't even known she possessed and it had all been for nothing. She just burst into wild, angry tears and ran for the steps.

'Stephanie!' Christian called to her but she just ignored him. He thought he was so clever! Naturally he hadn't taken her into his confidence. She was only Jean-Paul's aunt, a female and therefore a fool. She ran into the house and dodged out of sight as she saw Jean-Paul.

'You are crying, Stevie?' he asked worriedly but she made it to the stairs, not looking round as she ran up swiftly.

'Of course not,' she managed lightly. 'I'm covered with sand. I'm getting a shower. See you later.'

She didn't have to bother about his safety. Uncle Christian was out there with his sentries. Who needed her? She dived under the shower and wept copious tears of red-hot rage. Nobody had ever humiliated her so much. He had left her feeling like a child playing games and he had accused her of maiming his men. What if they had been the kidnappers? What then? He wouldn't be feeling so superior now!

She was too upset even to dry herself properly. She put on a bathrobe and padded into her bedroom, still sniffing with angry misery. Far from worrying about him, she could kill Christian herself. At the moment she felt that she couldn't face anything else and especially not him.

He was in her room, standing by her window, and she stopped as if she had been shot. It was just about the last straw. He had even dared to come into her room to chastise her further. There was no limit to his arrogance.

'Get out!' she shouted, pointing at the door. 'Out! Out! Out!'

'Calm down, Stephanie,' he ordered severely. 'You are shouting again.'

'Don't you tell *me* what to do, you chauvinistic French——!'

She didn't get any further; he took one stride forward and grabbed her, looking down at her furiously.

'One more word and I will silence you,' he threatened. 'Once again you have lost control of an obviously wild temper. You are yelling at me with no thought of Jean-Paul. Be sensible and I will discuss things with you.'

'It's too late to discuss things with me,' she shouted. 'You've just gone one step further to prove what you are. From now on I'll ignore everything you say!'

'Will you?' he asked angrily. 'We will see, *mademoiselle*. I told you to be silent.'

'You can——!' Stephanie began and that was as far as she got. Christian silenced her effectively by pulling her completely into his arms and crushing her lips with his.

CHAPTER FIVE

STEPHANIE was too shocked to struggle and by the time outrage replaced shock it was too late. She was locked in arms like steel and his mouth was ravaging hers with no chance of her escaping. It was something that had never happened to her before. She was used to looking with amusement on most men except close friends. Too many men had admired her and chased her and she had never had any trouble dispatching them. The kisses she had been given had been careful and sometimes almost apologetic. Christian was punishing her in a very masculine way and it was obvious that he felt nothing but contempt and rage.

He didn't stop until her knees were sagging and soft moans of anguish were reaching her own ears. When he lifted his head and stared down at her she felt completely weak, light-headed and dazed. She knew that if he let her go she would sink to the floor but he held on to her, mesmerising her with brilliantly blue eyes.

'Now will you listen to me?' he rasped.

'No.' She shook her head and stared back at him, summoning up every bit of defiance in her to get her out of this situation. She was trembling violently but there was nothing she could do about that. With a bit of luck, though, he might think it was rage and not the result of that devastating kiss.

'Stephanie!' he warned and she managed to hold her head up proudly.

'I refuse to speak to you,' she informed him in a shaking voice. 'You have no right to be in my room. When Thierry comes back I shall complain.'

'If he annoys me I will transfer him to the Arctic,' Christian threatened, watching her face with menacing, narrowed eyes.

'You wouldn't!' She was stunned at his cold assertion and he stared at her in exasperation, giving her a little shake.

'Of course I would not, you little *imbécile*. I'm not a villain.'

'You are,' she assured him shakily. 'I knew it as soon as I saw you and I'll never forgive you for what you've just done.'

His tight anger relaxed and his lips twitched with amusement.

'What have I done? Did I beat you?' he asked wryly. 'There must be an easy way to control you and perhaps I have found it. I am quite prepared to kiss you better, though.'

'Just let me go and kindly leave this room,' Stephanie said with shivering dignity. 'Nobody has ever behaved like that with me before.'

'Perhaps you have never infuriated anyone as you infuriate me,' he surmised. 'At least you are no longer shouting. Listen,' he added as she struggled to get free. 'I have two injured men in the kitchen at this moment. They will not be able to see properly for hours. Meanwhile, let me remind you that as you have maimed our allies we are on our own.'

'You're blaming me for this?' Stephanie asked angrily. 'You have two men sneaking about and because I imagine they're kidnappers and attack them you blame me? Why couldn't you have told me you had guards?'

'Because I did not trust you,' he admitted. 'I still do not. You cannot be relied upon to hold your tongue and this thing must be played out carefully or we lose.' He shrugged rather ruefully when she looked at him with accusing eyes. 'I do not doubt your commitment to Jean-Paul,' he assured her. 'Perhaps I should have told you, as things have worked out. However, I did not expect them to be seen. I also underestimated the extent of your courage and your capacity for combat. I imagined that any female who knew that guards were needed would be terrified.'

'Don't you think it's more frightening to imagine that only one man was protecting us?' Stephanie asked bitterly. 'I thought it was just us and them and I thought that nobody could help but you. No wonder you were content just to sit here. It's a pity I didn't know about your small army.'

'You think I am not capable of defending you?'

'I think you're capable of anything,' she assured him stiffly, pulling herself free of those dangerous arms. 'In fact I know you are. I would now like you to leave my room and please don't ever come into it again. Were it not for Jean-Paul I would leave St Lucien right now.'

'I can have you away within the hour,' he offered as he turned to the door and it was Stephanie's eyes that narrowed then.

'Oh, yes! You'd like that, wouldn't you?' she asked triumphantly. 'I can now see what the savage attack on me was about just now. You think you can frighten me, don't you? Well, you're wrong!'

'I did not do it to frighten you,' he assured her silkily, stopping to let his eyes drift over her. 'Believe me, the fear is all mine. You are delightful to hold. I could, with a little practice, become addicted to you.'

'Stick to Denise,' Stephanie snapped as she felt her face flush. 'You're a matching set, like two nasty bookends.'

'Come downstairs,' he ordered drily. 'Once again you have some explaining to do to your nephew. No doubt he is anxious about your shouting and worried about your certainty that two men were going to kill me. I can see that you are quite prepared to throw yourself in front of me to protect me too. Thank you, *mademoiselle*, but it will not be necessary.'

He closed the door and she scowled at it ferociously. There was no trick in the book he could pull that would take her in. From now on she would just ignore him and as soon as she could she would leave St Lucien. If she got the chance she would just go and take Jean-Paul with her.

She shook her head at the thought. Christian had the power to take care of him. Christian had the organisation and it was really his responsibility because all this was aimed at him. If he hadn't been so hideously chauvinistic she would have gladly co-operated; in fact she had really tried to. But now he had made it impossible and she would just have to watch over things by herself because it was obvious that if he hadn't told her that the place was guarded he was not about to tell her anything else. She was actually on her own. She would have to rely on her wits. She was sorry about the innocent men, but then, just how innocent were they as they were associated with Christian Durand? She just wished it had been him because no doubt Louisa would be the one administering to their needs and Louisa was about as gentle as a bear in thick gloves.

She went to dry her hair and saw her bruised lips. Her whole appearance made her cheeks flood with colour again. She had never looked so wild in her life and her limbs still felt peculiar, as if they didn't quite belong to her. She told herself firmly that it was the mad run up the beach and began to get ready to go down.

Tonight was definitely an image night, as cool an image as she could summon up. She ran her fingers over her lips, trying to take the feeling away but she could still smell his aftershave and he still seemed to be surrounding her. Hating him was a very good idea and she could hate just as well as anyone else.

The thought stopped her in her tracks and she stared worriedly at herself in the mirror. Before Christian came, she had never even been in a temper, let alone hated. She seemed to have spent her life laughing. Where had that gone now?

Downstairs, Jean-Paul was sitting on the settee, obviously waiting and obviously worried. He jumped up when she came in and looked at her closely.

'I heard you shouting, Stevie,' he confessed anxiously. 'Are you angry?'

'Not now,' she assured him, smiling at him and giving him a hug. 'It was just a little thing but it's gone now. In any case, I wasn't shouting at you so why worry?'

'You were shouting at Oncle Christian?' Jean-Paul asked, looking at her with a great deal of awe and admiration.

'She was shouting at me very loudly,' Christian informed him, coming in at that moment. 'It is all right now, though. She has forgiven me.'

Somewhat hampered by her nephew's presence, Stephanie had to let that one go and Jean-Paul's expression lightened.

'Oh,' he said with relief in his voice. 'Sometimes Maman and Papa shout at each other and then they are happy later. It is a lovers' quarrel, yes? Papa says so.'

'He is quite right,' Christian assured him smoothly. 'Stephanie is happy now.'

Jean-Paul set off towards the garden and Stephanie took a deep breath, ready to turn on Christian, but then the boy stopped and looked puzzled.

'Who were those two men on the beach, Stevie?'

'Oh, just men from Uncle Christian's boat. They're all right.'

'Then why did you run so fast to Uncle Christian and why did he hold you tight?'

'I was giving her a hug,' Christian admitted glibly and Jean-Paul looked at Stephanie in amazement.

'Then why were you shouting at him?' he wanted to know. She couldn't think of a single excuse but once again Christian stepped into the breach.

'She is very bad-tempered,' he admitted sadly.

Stephanie turned on him when Jean-Paul went out.

'I can see that you're a gifted liar,' she snapped, 'along with your other accomplishments.'

He gave her a very sardonic look and shrugged his shoulders.

'You wanted Jean-Paul to be alarmed?'

'It would have been possible just to pass it off easily without such elaborate embroidery,' she told him fiercely. 'There was no need to let him think that...'

'Ah! I see! The lovers' quarrel worries you. But why should it? It has made a little boy happy and, as you very well know, I am already part of a matching set, one of two nasty book-ends. You are quite safe, *mademoiselle*,'

He gave her a look that was very scornful and went to join Jean-Paul and this time Stephanie let him. For now, Christian had got the better of her and she would take a while to recover. She felt very badly shaken, though, what with one thing and another, and she was not looking forward to dinner and Denise.

She was determined not to speak to Christian unless it was absolutely necessary. In the event, he did not speak to her. He seemed to be musing over some problem and Stephanie assumed it was how to get rid of her. It was an uncomfortable meal with both Christian and herself trying to be normal for Jean-Paul's sake. He missed very little indeed and she rather felt that Christian also noticed the bright, dark eyes on them for most of the time.

Denise seemed reluctant to follow her usual pattern of disappearing to bed early. She was too interested in the way Stephanie and Christian were avoiding each other's eyes. It was making her suspicious and in the end Christian took a firm hold on the situation as Stephanie was about to leave.

'I would like to speak to you, Stephanie,' he said with very stiff courtesy. 'Perhaps you could excuse us, Denise? We will use the study.'

'Of course! I can easily occupy myself, Christian.' She smiled that brilliant smile and Stephanie wondered if she would occupy herself by listening at the keyhole. Not that it mattered. Any discussion with Christian was sure to be heated. Interested parties merely needed to stand in the garden.

'This cannot go on,' Christian stated severely when they were both safely in the comparative privacy of the study. 'I do not doubt that your motives are excellent but I cannot concentrate on Jean-Paul's safety while you are here.'

Stephanie sat down, staring up at him coldly. Here it was again. If one line of attack didn't succeed he tried another.

'I absolutely refuse to leave,' she said emphatically. 'If our positions were reversed you would refuse to leave too.'

'There is no comparison,' Christian bit out. 'I am a man. It gives me certain advantages.'

'I've already discovered that,' Stephanie snapped. 'You have sufficiently superior strength to assault people. The great advantage you have over me is physical. Your other advantage is wealth and if you didn't have so much of that commodity Jean-Paul wouldn't be under threat. I think instead of this attitude of supremacy you should be feeling a certain amount of guilt.'

'I am feeling a certain amount of fury!' Christian glared down at her frustratedly. 'Reasoning with you is enough to drive anyone mad. You flutter away from the point with astonishing skill. I assume it is deliberate, unless you are naturally stupid.'

'If you invited me into Thierry's study to insult me, then I think we can end this meeting,' Stephanie said tightly, standing up to leave. 'I should be watching Jean-Paul; so should you for that matter.'

'Very well,' Christian rasped. 'For the time being, I will let the matter go. In the meantime I will introduce you to our small army.'

He went to the door and called in the two men who had suffered from her attack on the beach and Stephanie could see the gleam of satisfaction in his eyes when she was obliged to explain and apologise. She knew he wanted to humiliate her but she refused to be embarrassed. She had been acting for the best and it was Christian's fault for not explaining.

Fortunately they took it well, even finding it amusing. They looked like tough men and apart from a slight redness about the eyes they seemed to have recovered.

'Will that be all?' Stephanie asked sharply when the men had gone and Christian stood looking at her steadily.

'For now. Tomorrow we will have to work out our immediate plan of action.'

'Very well.' Stephanie did not relax at all. She didn't trust him one bit.

'I shall have to take Denise into consideration,' he mused, half to himself, and Stephanie looked at him scornfully. He was still thinking about that woman when danger was swimming around them.

'Fortunately, she's your problem. I'll just go and peep in at mine.'

She wanted to walk past him but his hand came to her arm.

'I shall also be watching Jean-Paul,' he reminded her. 'Before you attack me, check my identification.'

Stephanie swept out, ignoring him, but she was perfectly well aware that he stood in the hall and watched her leave. It didn't matter, she was used to being watched, and she went gracefully up the stairs, never looking around.

In a way she had won because he had admitted that she was in this as a partner. If he had taken that attitude sooner she would have been glad but now she was just worried and rather depressed. Christian had unsettled her and angered her so much that she felt like another person. He had brought her out of the magic of this place and into reality with some speed. Her beautiful island was now a place of danger. She wanted to go home, but not without Jean-Paul.

'Ah! The discussion is over, Mademoiselle Caine?'

When Stephanie looked up from her gloomy reverie, Denise was standing watching her. She had her hand on the door of Christian's bedroom and it was quite clear that she had been just going in or just coming out.

'Completely over,' Stephanie assured her tightly. 'He's all alone if you wish to go down.'

'Oh, I think not. I am all ready for bed as you see. I'll just wait for him to come up.'

Stephanie did see. Denise was in a rather slinky satin *négligé*. It was a wild rose colour that contrasted beautifully with her dark hair and it didn't much matter whether she had been going out of or coming into Christian's room. Her plans for the night were already made.

'Why don't you go down and get a drink?' Stephanie asked waspishly. 'It will settle your nerves.'

'Christian will settle my nerves, *mademoiselle*,' Denise said with a satisfied smile. 'He usually does.'

Stephanie just walked into her room and closed the door firmly. Suspicion was now certainty. She got ready for bed slowly, trying to fight off a depression that had come when she had seen Denise. It angered her too. What did she care if Christian spent tonight and every night with his mistress? She hated him anyway.

She put her dressing-gown on and went to take a peep at Jean-Paul, almost bumping into Christian as he came along the passage.

'You may go to sleep,' he said curtly, his hand coming to her arm as she almost overbalanced in trying to avoid a collision. 'I will watch Jean-Paul.'

'You'll be otherwise occupied,' Stephanie snapped in a low voice. 'The cabaret is already in your room.'

'What are you talking about?' He swung her to face him, his hands none too gentle, and Stephanie wrenched herself free.

'I said my goodnights to Denise as she was going into your room,' she told him tersely. 'Even you can't be in two places at once, so I'll watch Jean-Paul. Or shall we split the time? I'll do ten until three and you can do three until six, when I'll be back on duty. After all, you'll need more sleep than I will.'

Christian turned and strode along to his room, flinging the door open and looking inside. He walked back out and looked at her with distaste.

'How odd that the room is empty,' he grated. 'Go to bed, *mademoiselle*. Content yourself with the knowledge that you have caused the maximum amount of trouble for one day. Start again tomorrow. Bearing this in mind, you will be the one to need the most sleep.'

'If she wasn't going in then she was just coming out,' Stephanie stated, her cheeks burning from his disgusted glance. 'I was talking to her.'

'Then she has all my sympathy,' he rasped. 'She was probably looking for a place to hide.'

He walked into his room and closed the door and Stephanie almost ran back to her own room. She felt like a wicked troublemaker even though she had most certainly seen Denise with her hand on Christian's door. She was probably in there right now, laughing. There was only Christian's word that the room had been empty. It had most likely been just a chance to make her feel foolish. He never missed out on things like that and she had walked right into it.

Next morning, Christian had a surprise for her. When she went down to breakfast Denise was already there and this unusual event assured Stephanie that something was happening. Jean-Paul was already out on the veranda and it seemed to her that Christian was deliberately getting him up early to have some time alone with him.

The night before was still very much at the top of her mind but she could see that this morning things were different. For a start, the two men sauntered on to the veranda and sat down by Jean-Paul and it was clear that they had new orders. She glanced in surprise at Christian and he was just waiting for that.

'Things are changed,' he said coolly. 'There is little point now in trying to maintain a low profile. We will have an obvious guard.'

Stephanie looked quickly at Denise but she was not at all put out by the revelations.

'I fully agree,' she said crisply. 'It is better to have an obvious guard. It will deter people.'

'I have explained things to Denise,' Christian said when Stephanie just stared at them both. 'She has agreed to leave today. It is the wisest thing to do. With three men to guard Jean-Paul there should be no trouble. A woman would be a problem that could upset everything. I would like you to leave with Denise, *mademoiselle*.'

Stephanie looked at him coldly. Another ploy to get rid of her! He was never going to stop.

'Are you issuing an order, *monsieur*?' she wanted to know. She went on looking at him. If he thought that yesterday's events had intimidated her he was mistaken. It had all been unforgivable and he should be cringing with shame, not sitting there delivering commands.

'I am suggesting that it would be wise,' he reminded her irritably. 'Denise sees the problem squarely and is leaving right away. She is going back to Martinique and there is no reason why you should not go there too. You could come back when this is over. Meanwhile I would, of course, pay your hotel bill.'

That merely added to Stephanie's annoyance. It was not helping either that Denise was listening to all this and was looking superior and smug, nodding her head sagely from time to time.

'Madame Pascal is not involved with this,' Stephanie pointed out sharply. 'Her reasons for being here in the first place are entirely different from mine. She is *your* guest and your problem. I am Jean-Paul's aunt and I was asked by his mother and father to be here and look after him. I am not about to leave until they come back.'

'If trouble comes you would merely be a complication!' Christian grated, frowning at her alarmingly. She was not alarmed. This was a sticking point and she had no intention of leaving.

'I am not deserting Jean-Paul,' she told him firmly. 'You may compare me with a fly in the ointment or a spanner in the works but here I am and here I stay.'

'I do not understand your peculiar English sayings,' he snapped. 'I can see, however, that when trouble comes I shall be expected to keep one eye on my nephew and the other on you.'

'I'll be busy keeping an eye on *my* nephew!' Stephanie seethed, standing and abandoning her breakfast. 'Meanwhile, I suggest you deal with the problem of Madame Pascal and keep out of my affairs!' She walked out angrily but she was not to be allowed to get away with things so easily. Christian followed her, taking her arm and marching her into the garden and away from prying eyes.

'I want you out of here!' he rasped, spinning her round as they reached the shelter of the flowering bushes that edged the lawn. 'If you do not come to your senses I may well resort to tying you up and getting that sack you spoke of. A woman is merely a liability in an affair like this. You proved that yesterday when you attacked two innocent men.'

'*And* got the better of them!' Stephanie reminded him angrily. She pulled free and stepped back, pointing her finger at him. 'Everything I've done wrong since you arrived has been your fault,' she accused. 'If you hadn't behaved like a tyrant I would never have tried to disobey. All you had to do right from the first was tell me the truth. You didn't do that because you're bursting with the force of your elevated ego. Get it into your head that I'm in this to the end. I have equal rights and equal responsibilities. Send your mistress to safety and leave me alone!'

He grasped her face in two hard hands, jerking her head up, but she refused to be scared. He was trying to kill her with blazing blue eyes but she glared right back even though she couldn't move an inch. It was difficult to move her mouth even but she would not be silenced.

'I'm not going,' she avowed through stiff lips that were hardly able to move. 'Violence will get you nowhere. We're in it together. Accept it.'

'When this is over, I will place you across my knee and enjoy beating some sense into you,' he growled in a low voice, letting her go and fixing her with a black frown.

'You probably mean some *respect*,' she answered tightly. 'People have to earn respect. I despise you, Monsieur Durand. You resort to violence with an ease that tells me it's second nature.'

He turned away in irritation.

'I am concerned for your safety,' he snapped. 'Situations like this are completely outside your comprehension. If anything happens to you I will never forgive myself.'

'Pigs might fly,' Stephanie remarked, adding immediately, 'Who was the telephone call from yesterday?'

Christian swung round and looked at her impatiently.

'It was merely from my office in Canada to let me know they had not located Thierry, and will you stop making these idiotic English remarks? I'm beginning to think that your intelligence is limited.'

'Sticks and stones,' Stephanie countered, marching back to the house with her head flung high.

He had tried again to get rid of her and once again he had failed. She knew perfectly well what he should do. He should take Jean-Paul out to his great big boat and prepare to repel boarders. Still, he probably had other tricks up his sleeve that he was keeping silent about and when she made a mistake it would be her fault again.

'If you imagine that flexing your muscles against a man such as Christian will make him find you attractive, you are very much mistaken.'

Stephanie looked up to find Denise standing halfway up the stairs, looking down at her scornfully.

'Christian likes femininity, not opposition,' Denise went on. 'You are constantly storming at him and he finds it distasteful. Staying here after I've gone is a waste of your time, Mademoiselle Caine. You will not be allowed to do as you wish. Christian will ignore you.'

'Then my prayers will have been answered!' Stephanie snapped. 'I'm staying here because Jean-Paul needs me and for no other reason. You're quite welcome to Monsieur Durand, don't worry.'

'I do not. I know him far too well to feel uneasy. When this is over he will come to Martinique for me.'

'I don't doubt it!' Stephanie snapped. 'This little problem of my nephew's safety must be a considerable inconvenience to both of you.'

'I have not been greatly inconvenienced,' Denise purred. 'I am here and Christian is here. I want little else.'

Stephanie walked off angrily and went to her own room to sit glowering out of the window. Jean-Paul was

with the two men, Christian was watching all of them.
There was really nothing she could do about it. She felt
restless and upset after her encounter with Denise and
she didn't feel as if she would ever smile again. Christian
had almost changed her character.

Denise went immediately after lunch. There was a
small airstrip that had several flights each day to the
bigger Caribbean islands and Christian took the Jeep to
drive Denise to the plane.

'May I come, Oncle Christian?' Jean-Paul asked
hopefully and Stephanie tightened up inside.

Without knowing it, Jean-Paul was playing right into
Christian's hands. He knew she would want to go too,
to be with her nephew, and he could so easily forbid it
because this was his last few minutes with Denise. In all
conscience she could not fuss and insist.

'Certainly you may come,' Christian assured him with
a smile. 'You can watch the planes, *n'est-ce pas*?' He
looked across at Stephanie with an unfathomable expression on his face. 'Of course,' he added softly, 'your
aunt Stephanie must come too. We are both responsible
for you and I would not like to leave her behind.'

'*Merveilleux*. It is an expedition after all, Stevie, and
I arranged it!' Jean-Paul exclaimed. He dashed off to
his room and Stephanie was left standing in front of
Christian with not a word to say. Now he had made her
feel slightly despicable for thinking maliciously about
him.

'I assume you would not have been happy to be left
behind?' Christian enquired coldly.

'I would not,' she assured him quietly. 'All the same,
I can't help wondering if it's sensible. There may be a
lot of people at the airstrip. There are plenty of buildings.
How do we know that... ?'

'We do not.' He turned away impatiently. 'Nor do we
know if they are on the beach, coming by boat or even
swimming. Some risks have to be taken.'

'Coming by boat?' Stephanie stared at him in alarm. 'I never thought of that.'

'Why not, *mademoiselle*?' he asked loftily. 'There are only two ways to come to St Lucien—by air or by sea. I have the airstrip watched. I cannot guard all the coastline. I have to rely on my instincts and my contacts. To go to the airstrip invites certain risks. To stay here invites more, to my way of thinking. I would not like anything to happen when I am away. That is why I came in the first place, to prevent trouble.'

'If you didn't have to take Madame Pascal...' Stephanie began reproachfully and he turned brilliantly angry eyes on her.

'If I do not send Denise away,' he pointed out icily, 'you may find yourself in the awkward position of being obliged to defend her. I believe you mentioned flinging yourself in front of her? If she is not here you will be able to use all your considerable skill in defending Jean-Paul. It is your stated aim, *mademoiselle*. As far as I am able to follow the trail of your logic, I am merely the muscle-power. When Denise is gone, I am at your disposal. No doubt you will inform me of my duties.'

He made her feel like a shrew and Stephanie blushed hotly.

'That's very unfair——' she began, but he interrupted coldly.

'*Naturellement*! It is the way of monsters. You expect anything else? Let us go, Mademoiselle Caine. We will keep an eye on our nephew and hope to get back unscathed.'

There was nothing that Stephanie could say. She felt completely put down and she had a sneaky feeling that she deserved it. Where the feeling had come from she did not know but it was there all the same.

They took the Jeep. Denise was placed securely in the front with Christian and Stephanie sat in the back with Jean-Paul. It was decidedly uncomfortable. The roads were not good and the Jeep was not the best of vehicles at any time. In the back, it was like torture. Not that Jean-Paul complained. He was happy and full of glee. To him this was an outing with his favourite people complete with added bonus—Madame Pascal was leaving. The shining dark eyes glanced in amusement at Stephanie.

'What did I tell you?' he whispered. 'She is going and now my prayers are answered. I have just you and Oncle Christian.'

Stephanie managed a smile but she was filled with unease. If her prayers had been answered there would be police surrounding Jean-Paul and the whole of St Lucien would be searched minutely, even under the stones. She could feel danger singing in the air and Christian seemed to be like a rock, immovable and cold.

He glanced at her in the mirror and their eyes met. With the sunlight on him he seemed more tanned, more sure of himself and those eyes were remarkable, blue as the sky. She just stared at him, almost without thought, unaware in her serious contemplation that he could see her too. The dark brows rose sceptically and she came to her senses, looking away rapidly with her cheeks flushed and hot. She was going out of her way to prove that she was slightly mad. His every expression told her so.

The road skirted the sea, climbing higher and then dropping to sea-level with speed. In between hanging on tightly and trying to talk to Jean-Paul, Stephanie had the urge to look back. She could hardly believe that after these few days they were at all safe. Whoever was coming would surely have come.

As they ascended the next rise, she glanced back again and her heart almost stopped at the sight of a car carefully trailing them. Of course, it might have been someone going in the same direction by sheer accident but Stephanie thought not. Apart from her shrieking instincts, this road was very sparsely travelled. The car was keeping just far enough back to be well away if they should stop.

She spun round and looked at Christian, her dark eyes wide open in alarm. Once again he was watching her through the mirror and he simply shook his head slowly. Stephanie understood without words. She was to say nothing. She couldn't in any case. It would alert Jean-Paul to danger. She started to turn again but once more Christian shook his head and she subsided without any further need of instruction. Christian was watching them. He had probably seen them well before she had and the realisation gave her an odd feeling of safety.

CHAPTER SIX

THE airstrip was a peculiar place. To the locals it was the airport but it could not be called that by any wild stretch of the imagination. There were a few sheds which might be called hangars but they were only capable of housing small planes. Even the larger planes that came here could not hold more than a few passengers because the airstrip itself was too small and too short. It served one purpose only—to ferry people to the larger islands where they could catch more sophisticated flights to faraway places.

There were a few shops, though, small wooden buildings clustered around the perimeter, and they did a good trade because flights came in regularly and the tourists always made straight for the place where a cold drink was waiting. The local traders were waiting too, smiling, merry and utterly beguiling. It was a good start for any holiday on St Lucien and if anything had been forgotten it was sure to be in one of the little cluttered shops.

Jean-Paul eyed them determinedly and showed Stephanie his small leather purse as Christian brought the Jeep to a stop.

'I collected my money,' Jean-Paul said quietly. 'First I will watch the plane. Then I will go to the shops. You think Oncle Christian will object?'

'I don't see why he should.' Stephanie pondered. Christian was fairly easygoing with his nephew. 'We'll all go together after Madame Pascal leaves.'

Jean-Paul looked a bit dubious about that but he turned to watch Denise Pascal checking over her many pieces of luggage and to Stephanie he looked as frosty as his French uncle.

'I will watch her fly off,' he said firmly and she could see that he didn't much care if it was on a broomstick. Jean-Paul wanted to see the last of Denise as much as she did. Denise was not a woman to endear herself to any child and she had not endeared herself to Stephanie either. She watched Christian with her and tried to solve the minor mystery of why he was at all interested in a woman who behaved like an ice queen. She must have something going for her and Stephanie could only assume it was physical. The thought almost made her shudder.

They all went to see the plane take off and Stephanie tried not to look when Denise wrapped her arms round Christian and kissed him lingeringly. Fortunately, Jean-Paul was watching the plane taxiing forward and Stephanie was quite glad about that. It would have been difficult to explain the affectionate farewell when not too long ago Christian had been explaining why he had held Stephanie. It might have given Jean-Paul a distorted idea of why she was supposed to have been in a rage.

It was hot on this flat land and after a minute or two Stephanie turned to Jean-Paul to ask if he shouldn't put his white hat on instead of carrying it. To her horror, he was not there. Seconds before, it seemed, he had been standing right beside her, watching the small silver plane take on its passengers. Now he was nowhere to be seen.

'Jean-Paul!' She shouted his name in a panic but the aircraft was turning to take off, the noise was loud and the dust was blowing across from the strip, swirling her skirts around her, getting in her eyes. She shouted again and then started to run. She had no idea where she would run to but she knew he couldn't be far. Whoever had him must still be in sight, even if they had made it to the sheds.

Fierce hands grabbed her arms and she was forced to stop quite violently.

'Where is Jean-Paul?' Christian gripped her cruelly and glared down at her as she turned her head. 'All you had to do was watch him for a few minutes! Where is he?'

'I—I don't know. He was there, right beside me and then when—when I looked again...'

'Let's go!' He just snapped out the words and then propelled her forward but Stephanie needed no urging. She raced across to the sheds, intending to search each one at some speed. Christian, though, did not accompany her and when she came from the first shed he was walking towards her, a puzzled Jean-Paul by his side.

It was such a relief that Stephanie simply stood and watched them, her whole body shaking. Then she sat down on the nearest object, too shocked to stand any longer. For a few minutes she had really thought that her blackest nightmares had come true, but he was here, walking along beside Christian, two bags clutched in his hand, and Christian was observing her as if she was a useless fool at the best and bordering on criminal at the worst.

'Stevie!' As she sat there trembling, Jean-Paul detached himself from Christian and ran forward. 'What is it? Are you going to cry?'

'She is not. I believe, though, that she imagined you had smuggled yourself onto the plane,' Christian said smoothly, pulling Stephanie to her feet and glancing at her closely.

'With Madame Pascal? As if I...' Jean-Paul stopped and looked worriedly at his uncle but Christian ignored the slip. Instead he took Stephanie by one arm and picked Jean-Paul up in the other.

'*Tout va bien*,' he assured them both. 'We will now go home.'

Stephanie was frantically trying to wipe at her moist eyes and control her shaking and Jean-Paul went unexpectedly red in the face.

'I am too old to be carried, Oncle Christian,' he pointed out in embarrassment and Christian immediately lowered him to his feet.

'I beg your pardon,' he said quietly. 'In my desire to get Stephanie to the Jeep I quite forgot your age. She has, however, been very worried about you. It would help perhaps if you held her hand.'

Jean-Paul didn't mind that at all and he came at once to take Stephanie's hand, looking up at her anxiously.

'I only went to the shops, Stevie,' he pleaded. 'It was a secret and I wanted to get there before you came with Oncle Christian.'

'If you'd just told me, instead of simply disappearing, I would have come and waited outside with my eyes shut,' Stephanie told him in a choked voice.

'I'm sorry. But I am here now,' Jean-Paul pointed out logically. 'In any case, the surprise is spoiled because Oncle Christian caught me.'

'I saw nothing at all,' Christian assured him as they came to the Jeep. 'If it is for your aunt, I hope it is truly a surprise and not another shock.'

'There is one each,' Jean-Paul stated and Christian boosted him into the back of the Jeep.

'Then sit there alone and peer into your paper bags. Your aunt will sit with me in a little more comfort.'

They pulled away and Stephanie settled back, her shaking legs returning to normal.

'I shouldn't have let it happen,' she whispered but Christian surprised her by looking merely amused.

'While you were watching for the enemy,' he said quietly, 'your charge was stealing away with great skill and the speed of small, untiring legs. Forget it. He is safe.'

Stephanie felt grateful that he was not reprimanding her and the thought of safety brought back the memory of the car following them.

'That car...' she began, glancing anxiously at Christian.

'My two men,' he assured her calmly.

'But I thought... You said you hadn't a car!'

'One was hired last night. I knew we would have to come to the plane and thought it better to have an escort.'

'And of course you never considered telling me,' Stephanie muttered in a crestfallen way.

'Did I have the opportunity, *mademoiselle*? You have spent the intervening time either flying at me in a rage or sticking so closely to your charge that I would have had to pass you a secret note.'

'When you just shook your head I thought...'

'I could not roar the information to you. Jean-Paul would have been intrigued; moreover, I did not want Denise to know.'

'Why?' Stephanie asked, instantly intrigued herself. He glanced across at her, his gaze running over her face and the still-wet shine of her dark eyes.

'She is easily upset—delicate,' he murmured ironically. 'On the other hand, I keep secrets from everyone. Choose whichever explanation suits you best.'

'In other words, mind my own business!' Stephanie snapped, tearful feelings quickly ebbing away.

'That is one way of looking at it,' he agreed smoothly. Stephanie looked straight ahead and closed her lips firmly. For a few minutes back there she had felt grateful to him but any sign of compassion with Christian Durand was merely the forerunner of disdain. He was totally given up to power and she could still feel that tight, hurtful grip on her arm when he had grabbed her at the airstrip.

She looked down at the red marks that still lingered, rubbing them surreptitiously.

'I am sorry,' he admitted softly. 'I did not mean to hurt you. I know you are diligent in your desire to protect Jean-Paul and I also admit that I have been perhaps a little hard on you. In your own world you are no doubt beautiful, cool and efficient. The circumstances here have thrown us both off-balance.'

'Not you, surely?' Stephanie asked, trying to come to terms with this confession—if that was what it was.

'I am not invincible.'

'I hope you are,' Stephanie breathed solemnly, looking across at him with serious dark eyes. 'It seems to me that your invincibility is all that's standing between Jean-Paul and disaster.'

'It is not a good idea to place your faith in another person,' Christian warned darkly. 'When it comes down to it, you have only yourself.'

'And what about Jean-Paul?'

'He is a child. It is different. Fortunately, we both love him.'

Stephanie held her shining hair back against the wind and looked at Christian closely, not at all sure as to what he meant. He certainly loved Jean-Paul. It was becoming very obvious. Still, it didn't excuse his desire to take a small boy from his parents.

She saw him glance in the mirror and instantly she was alert.

'It is all right,' he assured her quietly. 'My men have pulled in behind us.'

'Where were they when Jean-Paul disappeared?' she asked wryly and his lips tightened although he never looked at her.

'They were being discreet, following orders,' he said tightly. 'I did not want them to be seen. Now it does not matter.'

Stephanie asked herself why. The only difference in the situation was that Denise had gone. Had he really meant it when he had said that he didn't want Denise

to know? She glanced at him but one look at his face
was enough to tell her that she would not be enlightened
even if she questioned him for hours.

'What are you talking about?' Jean-Paul wanted to
know, leaning forward to push his head as closely to
them as possible.

'We are planning a little excitement,' Christian said
unexpectedly. 'You have finished looking into your paper
bags, I assume?'

'*Oui*. I am very satisfied!' Jean-Paul said promptly
and Christian's lips quirked at the pleased tone.
Stephanie felt a wave of annoyance. It was like a game.
Jean-Paul didn't know a thing about the danger and even
if he did he was young enough to treat it as an adventure. Christian ranged from cold anger to sardonic
amusement. Was she the only one feeling scared?

There had been many firsts since she had met Christian
Durand. She had been almost constantly in a rage, she
had been flung into one panic after another and now
she was just shakily scared. He had a lot to answer for
because he was entirely to blame. If he had been at all
reasonable she would never have raged at him. If he had
explained things to her and taken the appropriate action
she would not have had need to panic. And if he hadn't
been so disgustingly rich none of this would have
happened.

She shot him an extremely irritated look and he
glanced at her in sceptical astonishment, one dark brow
raised, and she got the silent message—her insanity was
showing! Stephanie wasn't surprised. When this was all
over she would be a completely changed character and
that was the most annoying thing of all. Until she had
met Christian she had been well content with her
character and with her life. It would be a struggle to get
back into her old carefree ways because she knew quite
well that the infuriating French face would linger in her
mind for the rest of her life.

*   *   *

Very late in the night, Stephanie awoke because of some noise that was now only a vague memory in her mind. She had been sleeping badly since Christian had come to St Lucien and now, with the added worry about Jean-Paul's safety, it took little to disturb her.

She sat up in bed listening, wondering if it had been footsteps or the last sound of the telephone. There was only one phone in the house and that was in Thierry's study, quite a way off. Of course, it might have been Christian looking in on Jean-Paul but he was usually very quiet. Whatever it was she was too anxious simply to go back to sleep and ignore it.

She got up and put on her wrap and went quietly to the door. When she looked into Jean-Paul's room, he was sleeping peacefully and that left the thought of someone downstairs. It might be Christian or it might be an intruder. Whoever it was she had to look or sit up all night on guard. She went softly to the stairs and she was halfway down, going very secretly, when Christian started to come up.

He looked up when he heard her little gasp and instead of speaking he stood watching her for a minute, his silence disconcerting her. Those blue eyes always seemed to pin her fast, very often leaving her unable to move at all.

'What is it?' When he finally spoke, Stephanie almost jumped at the sound of his voice. She had been staring at him so raptly that she had trouble adjusting to the present.

'Something disturbed me. I had to get up and look.'

He nodded in understanding and motioned her to come down.

'It was probably the telephone. It is just as well because I would have had to tell you tomorrow. As you are awake we can talk now. Come down and have a coffee.'

She could see that whatever the phone message was about it had stunned him into this mood of near-affability and it only put her more on edge.

'Was it about Fiona and Thierry?'

As she got to the bottom of the stairs, Stephanie stopped to look up at him and Christian made no attempt to dodge the issue.

'Yes. They have been found. Come into the kitchen and I will make coffee. We can talk there.'

'Are they coming back now?' Stephanie found herself in the position of having to drag information out of him yet again. He had decided exactly where he would talk and it certainly was not going to be in the hall. 'Are they coming back?' she persisted.

'No.' Having made it to the kitchen, Christian closed the door firmly and turned to look at her. 'They cannot. Fiona is in hospital. I spoke to Thierry.'

Stephanie sat on the nearest chair, shocked by the news. She couldn't think of a thing to say. Whatever she had imagined it was it would never have been the thought of Fiona being ill. As far as she could remember, Fiona had never been ill in her life. Being ill in bed meant that she missed out on things and Fiona had never been one to miss anything at all.

'What's wrong with her?' Stephanie whispered, knowing it must be something dreadful.

'An accident.' Christian glanced at her and handed her a steaming cup of coffee. 'Drink this. You look shaken but there was no easy way to tell you. You would like me to get you a brandy?'

Stephanie shook her head and went on staring at him, ignoring the drink in her hand, and he began to pace about, his brows drawn together in a frown.

'Your sister is very adept at getting her own way,' he murmured irritably. 'I have known this for some time but I must confess that I am surprised by this turn of events. It does not seem at all like her.'

'Why? I—I don't know what you're talking about...'

'Apparently, your sister had the greatest desire to see the real north, the true wilderness,' Christian informed her, giving her a suspicious look as if she had been party to this unexpected plot. 'As usual, Thierry indulged her. He seems to be incapable of saying no to her.'

'It's called love,' Stephanie muttered vaguely.

'Is it?' Christian grated. 'I had always thought that love protected. Now he has let her be endangered. A strange kind of love, *mademoiselle*. To me it sounds more like a simple inability to say no firmly.'

'Will you please tell me what happened?' Stephanie begged. 'If you want to fight I'll oblige you later but I want to know about Fiona.'

'I have no desire to fight with you.' Christian pulled up a chair, straddling it and sitting with his arms along the back as he gazed at Stephanie. 'You are fond of Fiona, are you not?'

'Of course I am! She's my sister. Tell me what happened, *please*!'

'Initially, they went with an organised party, properly equipped, a guide to help them and everything was fine. Later, though, they branched out on their own, Fiona following her desire to confront the wilderness. For a few days, nobody knew where they were. No search was organised because they had made it quite plain that they meant to be alone. They had maps and a master plan,' he added disgustedly. 'Unfortunately, your sister fell and injured her leg. Then they had trouble. Thierry dared not leave her and nobody came to find them. By the time that somebody did, Fiona was suffering from more than a broken leg. They were out in the open in a tent, romantic but impractical. She is in hospital, exposure adding to her problems. According to Thierry, she will be there for at least two weeks.'

'Is she all right, though?' Stephanie forgot who this was and in her anxiety she gripped his hand as it lay along the back of the chair.

'She will be.' The long brown fingers closed over hers warmly. 'Thierry is there and he seems well satisfied with the care she is getting. His call of course was to you. He did not expect to find me here.'

'Oh!' Stephanie looked up at him and met the brilliant blue gaze. 'What about—about . . . ?'

'That is why I need a discussion with you,' Christian said seriously. 'Do we tell them about Jean-Paul? Do we let them know that their son is in danger? If we do, what are Thierry's options?'

Stephanie knew exactly what he meant. If Thierry knew, he would want to come back and Fiona could not come. She would be sick with worry, the last thing she needed when she was ill. Thierry too would be torn between hurrying back and staying with his wife. They would be separated by thousands of miles and Thierry would be no more able to protect his son than she was. When it was all weighed up, it was Christian who would protect Jean-Paul.

Involuntarily, Stephanie's fingers tightened around Christian's as she looked up at him. There was nothing for it but to take the very serious responsibility of keeping this from Fiona and Thierry.

'We'll have to deal with this ourselves,' she said quietly. 'Thierry can't be in two places at once and if he leaves Fiona he will have to have a good reason. To tell her the truth will have her insisting on coming too and that would be a bad idea, even if she could manage it. It might be wrong of us, but I don't think we should tell them.'

'*D'accord*! I have reached the same conclusion. I am glad that you agree.' He looked at her closely and smiled, a brief twisting of his long lips. 'I am surprised that you agree, however. May I know the mental process that has brought you to this decision?'

'Thierry can't leave Fiona without adequate explanations,' Stephanie said solemnly. 'It would only make her worse. And if he came, what could he do? He might even be in the way.'

'In the way? He is the boy's father.'

'But he's not like you,' Stephanie pointed out earnestly. 'I prayed for them to come back when I knew about this but I changed my mind almost straight away.'

'Why?' Christian eyed her narrowly and Stephanie looked down at their joined hands. She had forgotten to pull away and he had not let go.

'Because if anyone can protect Jean-Paul, it has to be you,' she assured him seriously. 'You're clever and—and tough and ... different.'

'Is this a compliment, *mademoiselle*?' he asked softly and Stephanie glanced up at him.

'I suppose it is. It doesn't cancel out your faults, though,' she added hastily.

'And they are many, as we know.' He gave a low laugh and raised her hand to his mouth, kissing the palm before letting it go. Stephanie was startled at the wave of electricity that seemed to shoot up to her shoulder but before she could do more than absorb the feeling he had stood, swinging the chair away and going to pour coffee for himself.

She just stared at the tall, dark figure, the lean hips and broad shoulders, the way his hair shone in the light, a strange presentiment touching her mind. At that moment she felt that her life would be deeply connected with this powerful man. It was almost a sense of destiny, a peculiar awareness that was heightened by the warm feeling where his lips had touched her skin.

He turned and she looked quickly away but she need not have bothered, Christian was back to normal, organised and decisive.

'*Alors*!' he growled. 'Tomorrow, we go to the boat. There is no longer any need to stay here. The guards are out in the open and Denise has gone.'

'You mean—you mean we would have gone straight to the boat if she hadn't been here?' Stephanie asked slowly, astonishment on her face.

'As you pointed out before, it is the obvious place to be.'

'Then why haven't we been there all the time?' Astonishment was fading and annoyance was beginning to shine from her dark eyes, a thing he noted immediately.

'Denise is not at all comfortable on a swaying deck,' he informed her with smooth mockery. 'As I have told you before, she is delicate.'

Stephanie rose, looking at him with distaste. Once again he was proving that he thought of that woman's comfort before the safety of his nephew.

'Goodnight, *monsieur*,' she snapped. 'I withdraw my compliment.'

She walked to the door, not looking back, but his darkly amused voice followed her.

'I expected it, therefore it is no great disappointment. *A bientôt*, Stephanie.'

She never bothered to answer. So much for presentiments, so much for trust and destiny. She had been right about him from the first and why she was feeling disappointed she had no idea. None of this was a surprise. She had worked it all out specifically as soon as she had seen him with Denise Pascal.

She thought of their lingering goodbye kiss and her lips tightened. No wonder she still had the warm feeling in the palm of her hand. She had encountered an expert. She got into bed and closed her eyes firmly. When his face floated into her mind she shut it out as viciously as she could.

Next day Christian was utterly in charge. By the time Stephanie came down, the whole day had been organised and there was nothing she could do to interfere, not that she would have even considered such a thing. In any case she had enough to do as it was.

'I have informed Jean-Paul that we are moving to the boat and naturally he is delighted,' Christian said as Stephanie sat down to her breakfast. 'I have also been in touch with Thierry.'

Stephanie looked up quickly. It was astonishing how guilty she felt about keeping this from Thierry and Fiona and for one minute she hoped that Christian had told his brother.

'What did he say? Did you tell him?'

'I told him we were moving back to the boat. I also told him that we may take a short cruise. He was relieved that Jean-Paul is being taken care of and that we have joined forces.' His dark brows drew together and he turned his considerable force of character on her. 'If you mean, did I tell him about the danger, then no, I most certainly did not. I understood that we were agreed on that subject, *mademoiselle*.'

'I know,' Stephanie sighed. 'This morning, though, I seem to be filled with guilt about it.'

'Clear your conscience. I will take the responsibility,' Christian snapped.

'It's not that at all, and you would know it if you weren't so unbending,' Stephanie retaliated angrily. 'Just stop treating me like the opposition. All that's troubling my conscience is the question of our right to do this—although I don't expect we have much choice really,' she added more quietly, calming down. 'Anyway, if Fiona came back, even in good health, she would interfere and fuss. She's better off out of it,' she finished.

When she looked up, Christian was sitting with his elbows on the table, his chin resting in his hand as he regarded her steadily. There was also a wicked gleam in his eyes.

'Your thought processes fascinate me,' he murmured, staring at her mockingly. 'I have just listened to you as you meandered from guilt and doubt to justification and certainty. It took about four sentences. You would make a fine commanding officer.' He grinned and leaned back. 'As to Fiona, I agree with you. We already have trouble and Fiona is better several thousand miles away. When it is all over, she can have one of her attacks.'

'She doesn't have attacks in actual fact,' Stephanie assured him glumly, still filled with doubts. 'It's all put on to get her own way. She's always been like that, even as a child.'

'Did she cause you trouble, *petite*?' Christian asked softly and Stephanie shook her head.

'No. It's always been a laugh. I know how to handle her.' She looked up suddenly. 'I think I would prefer to remain as *mademoiselle*. It has a cold ring the way you say it and it fits the picture better. We're temporary allies but I don't expect it to last.'

Christian stood and glanced down at her sardonically.

'I apologise, *mademoiselle*. There are occasions when you quite touch my heart and our dislike of each other slips my mind. I will take care in future.'

He walked out and Stephanie realised he hadn't told her one thing to do. Well, she wasn't going to ask him. There was the packing for a start and she imagined that Jean-Paul would want to take something to do on board. If it hadn't been for the danger and if it hadn't been for Christian she would be quite excited about it all.

She admitted secretly that in fact she was excited. This sunny morning, with the men planted firmly outside the house and everything calm, danger seemed remote. There was the feeling of a holiday in the air and, even though it was a feeling that would go very swiftly, she had to acknowledge that it was there at the moment.

After breakfast, when she was crossing the hall, Christian came in and she turned to him without any rancour at all.

'I'm going to pack for Jean-Paul and me,' she confided. He just looked at her and she stopped dead as a thought struck her. 'Will we be coming back here at all?'

'Who knows?' He gave one of those easy shrugs and added nothing to help.

'Well...' Stephanie pondered. 'I was wondering about taking all my things, actually. When the danger is over, I'll be going back to London. I was supposed to have a few weeks off and then I have assignments.' She looked up quickly. 'And don't start trying to get rid of me again!'

'How can someone so beautiful be so bad-tempered?' Christian mused mockingly. 'I never for one moment considered getting rid of you. I am about to show you my yacht. What happens later we shall see but take your luggage by all means.'

'I've seen your yacht before,' Stephanie confessed perkily, stopping at the bottom of the stairs to turn to him. 'I was here when I was nineteen and you sailed into the bay. It all looked beautiful and romantic. I was watching with Thierry's binoculars and in fact I saw you too as you came on deck.'

'So you knew who I was when I arrived this time?' Christian questioned with suddenly narrowed eyes.

'No. As a matter of fact, it took a minute or two. When I saw you before you looked different—kind, amused, very pleasant. Of course it was all from a distance. Characters are much more easily assessed from close quarters.' She was pleased with her sarcasm until Christian took two steps forward and caught her by the waist with strong hands.

'The closer the quarters, the better the assessment,' he murmured ironically as she gasped and struggled. 'Do not bandy insults with me, *mademoiselle*,' he warned quietly. 'When I run out of words, I resort to action. In any case,' he finished, letting her go and turning away, 'I did not then have quite so many responsibilities and I was amused to find myself under observation from the house on that occasion. It may have accounted for my kindly appearance. When you had finished observing me, I did some observing of my own. There are also binoculars on the yacht and I had a close look at the silver-haired girl who was so interested. I thought you looked delightful. Which proves your own conclusion: characters are better assessed from close quarters.'

He walked off, leaving Stephanie red-faced. Her little dig at him had once again gone amiss. He was better avoided but that was going to be impossible now. She wondered how long this stay on the boat would be. Surely by now they had some idea of the whereabouts of the kidnappers? It was difficult to believe that Christian hadn't already got them under lock and key.

Stephanie bit her lip when she realised that she was giving him almost superhuman powers. He was just like any other rich man. Even as she thought it she shook her head. He wasn't. He was the nearest thing to raw power she had ever met and if he had been nice with it he would have been fascinating. However, he was definitely not nice and he was already fascinating to Denise Pascal. When her mind began to wander to his life away from the island, she dropped the thought swiftly.

Christian's boat was called the *Sea Queen* and it was certainly more grand than Stephanie had ever imagined. They came on board in the late afternoon. Christian drove them over to the cove and a launch came out from the yacht to meet them. She realised he had some way of communicating with his crew and it was something she should have known all the time. Of course someone like Christian would never cut himself off from his responsibilities whether it was his great boat or his business interests. Already, as he had told her, somebody was on the way to Canada to take over Thierry's duties.

She was surprised that she had not seen the yacht when she and Jean-Paul had come to the cove on Christian's second day on the island, but now she knew why. It was anchored out of sight but as the launch came in to collect them the great white boat came into view around the headland like some awesome mythological creature. The fact that it was silent and under sail added to the mystery of it and Stephanie gazed in wonder.

'She is beautiful, yes?' Christian had noticed her face and asked the question in a low voice, not spoiling the moment for her, and Stephanie was grateful.

'It almost looks as if it's come from the clouds,' she said in a whisper, never taking her eyes from it.

'Once on board you will change your mind,' he assured her with a quiet laugh. 'Everything is modern. When the sails come down too, the illusion vanishes.'

She was rather glad about that because her mind had once again gone back to pirates and she felt a surge of irritation with herself. She knew exactly what Christian Durand was and it was not some romantic pirate from a child's dream.

It was rather exhilarating riding out to the boat and Jean-Paul never spoke at all. Like Stephanie, he was filled with awe. The crew were watching them approach and Stephanie shot a quick glance at Christian as she saw the men waiting.

'Hand-picked,' he said shortly before turning away. He had not needed words from her and she knew in any case that he would have a crew who were utterly trustworthy. She wondered what they thought of this situation, one woman on board on the outward journey and a different one now. It brought her mind back to Denise

Pascal and the excitement died from her eyes. By the time they stepped on board, Stephanie was composed and perfectly straight-faced and if Christian noticed he said nothing in his usual way.

CHAPTER SEVEN

SETTLING Jean-Paul that night was not easy. Nothing had happened to quell his excitement and he wanted to spend the night looking out of the porthole and watching the sea, or so he told her. Finally, however, sleep overcame him and Stephanie dressed with care for her first dinner alone with Christian.

'How many are on board?' she asked as she accepted a drink in the glitter of the saloon as they waited for dinner.

'Five. The yacht is big and takes a fair amount of handling. I even have a captain.' Christian said this with a wry smile and Stephanie was not left in doubt of his word for long because the captain joined them for dinner. He was a tough-looking Frenchman who could also have joined her pirate scenario. He was quite charming, though, and before the meal was over she was glad of his company.

Michel Arlaud was in his early thirties, obviously used to the sea and as fair as Christian was dark.

'It is a pleasure to have such delightful company, *mademoiselle*,' he assured Stephanie when Christian introduced them. 'To a long voyage,' he saluted as he was handed a drink.

'Do you spend all your time on board the *Sea Queen*?' Stephanie asked, and he smiled at her in a rather indulgent manner.

'I would like to, but Monsieur Durand spends little time on her himself. When I am not being grand, giving orders and dining at the owner's table, I am a poor fisherman.'

It seemed unlikely and Christian shot her an amused look as she pondered the statement.

'Michel owns a small fishing fleet,' he corrected. 'He is speaking in this manner to impress you. I have known him for a long time and he invariably calls me Christian. He runs the *Sea Queen* for me because he likes sailing and cannot quite afford a boat of this size himself. He also likes trouble,' Christian added quietly.

She could believe that. One glance at the wry grin on Michel Arlaud's face assured her that he would just love trouble.

'I'm glad he's on our side,' she told Christian later as the captain went back to his duties and they were left alone. 'Does he...? Do the crew know that...?'

'They do. I have had them with me for many years and Michel and I were at school together. He is younger than I but even then he was not given to compromise. He doesn't need this job, he just likes the challenge of sailing. We are in little danger here.'

Naturally Stephanie wanted to ask why they hadn't come here in the first place, but then she remembered his sardonic remarks about Denise's delicacy and decided to be silent on the subject.

'What about the two who were at the house?'

'They are not part of the crew. They flew over from Paris as soon as I knew there would be trouble. I have left them to guard the house for the time being. They are more use to us on shore and in any case there is not room for them on board. When everything is over, they will fly home.'

'When is it going to be over?' Stephanie sighed, sitting back against the luxurious cushions and looking gloomily into her drink.

'Perhaps sooner than you think,' Christian surmised quietly. In the glitter of the lamplight, her hair was astonishingly fair, silver-gilt, cascading around her shoulders and brushing against a perfect skin. He watched her for a second and then volunteered further information.

'I have told Thierry that I am taking Jean-Paul back to Paris with me. It will give him a holiday and he will be able to take a look at his new school.'

'What did Thierry say to that?' Stephanie asked. She noted that he had *told* Thierry, not asked him if it would be all right. When Jean-Paul finally went to school in Paris, Thierry and Fiona could bid him a fond farewell because Christian would take over completely. Fiona had been quite right.

'He thought it was an excellent idea. Fiona can now recover in tranquillity. They know exactly where Jean-Paul is and whom he is with.'

Yes. Stephanie could quite see that. In Paris he would be with his uncle and he would certainly not be with his aunt because she could not force her way there to insist on her equal role and equal rights. No doubt Christian had all this well thought out.

'So when do we sail off?' she asked rather bitterly and Christian looked at her with narrowed eyes that were as glittering as the lights.

'When there is no more danger. When the villains are captured. Until then, we stay right here, well away from the shore, completely safe. We watch and we wait.'

'I expect they'll be doing exactly the same thing,' Stephanie pointed out stiffly and his eyes narrowed even further as he regarded her with slow interest.

'I think not. The net is in place. They will walk right into it and it will not be long.'

'How do you know?' Stephanie leaned forward and stared at him with almost the same awe on her face that had been there when she had first seen the boat.

'Because I have been studying their methods for some time. It was, after all, only a matter of time before they turned their attentions to me. I do not believe in being caught, how do you say, left-footed? I know how they work, I even have a good idea of how they think. When you are in the head of the quarry, the trap is easy to set. It is set, *ma chère*. We now listen for the sound of a struggle.'

'You're rather frightening,' Stephanie pronounced quietly and he made a wry face, standing and pulling her to her feet.

'Perhaps to my enemies I am. I have few enemies, however, no matter how unlikely you find that idea. Someone who wishes to hurt those who belong to me are enemies and are likely to find little mercy.' He glanced down at her and suddenly smiled. 'You are not an enemy, Stephanie. Sleep in peace. There will be no need whatever to pace the boat with your hairdrier at the ready.'

'I wasn't going to,' she protested, blushing when he interrupted with,

'*Bien*! I am pleased to hear it. You tend to do your creeping about with little more to cover you than a fascinating piece of skimpy silk. The crew are serious men and I would like them to remain so. Our safety depends on it.'

Stephanie spun round to march off. She could do little else because he had caught her more than once in what she imagined he would term provocative attire. It had all been an accident but he would not think that.

'*Bonsoir, petite*.' Before she could escape, Christian caught her shoulders and spun her round and while she was still shaken by surprise his lips covered hers in a kiss that was as gentle as his first kiss had been fierce. There was nothing of the chastising attention he had forced on her before and when he lifted his head she was quite still, gazing at him with dark eyes that held puzzlement and regret.

'Why did you do that?' She could only ask in a fretful way because it just wasn't fair. She would have liked that goodnight kiss if it had been genuine, if there had not been the thought in her mind of him kissing Denise here and then going with her to his cabin.

'Because I wished to,' he said softly, his hand still tilting her face. 'I have sunk into the despicable ways of the very wealthy, as you no doubt realise. The habit of doing what I want is now firmly entrenched. I wanted to kiss you and I can still see no reason why I should not have followed my inclinations.'

'How would you feel if I followed my inclinations and slapped your face hard?' Stephanie asked shakily.

'I would not be pleased and I would probably retaliate swiftly.' He put his head on one side and looked at her quizzically. 'You may do it if you like. If that is really your uppermost thought.'

Stephanie walked off. It was not her uppermost thought and she suspected that he knew it only too well. For a minute, her uppermost thought had been to linger and feel again the gentle brushing of his lips against hers. It had given the same tingling of electricity that his kiss on her palm had done, a feeling that was quite new to her.

She had never met a dangerous male before and Christian was total danger. He ruled by wealth and power but even without it he would be awe-inspiring. Add to that his breathtaking masculinity and he was too daunting for words. She was glad to get to her cabin and lock the door, even more alarmed when she realised that there was absolutely no need to lock it. He was, among other things, completely trustworthy.

She undressed and then spent a considerable time simply looking out at the sea, as Jean-Paul had done. There was a bright moon and the light caught the white tops of the gentle waves that broke on the shoreline of the cove. It was almost impossible to imagine danger in such peace and beauty but she never doubted that it was there. She never doubted either that Christian was ready for it and would vanquish anyone who ventured forth. Already the net was prepared; he had said so.

She shivered in spite of the warm evening and climbed into her bed, letting the almost imperceptible rocking of the boat soothe her. What would tomorrow bring and the day after? How long would they be here? And how often would she be able to see Jean-Paul when he was firmly in Christian's hands, living in Paris and being turned into another being she would eventually not recognise?

Christian should have children of his own, and why hadn't he? His children would be dark, handsome and greatly loved. His affection for his nephew showed that he would love his own children dearly. Denise already had children. Did he see them? Did he feel the same affection for them that he felt for Jean-Paul?

Stephanie turned restlessly, annoyed with herself for this wild imagining that threatened to bring her to the edge of tears. It was none of her business, nothing to do with her at all. If it had not been for the threat to Jean-Paul, Christian would never have come to St Lucien and she would probably never have met him in the whole of her life.

That was not a pleasing thought either and Stephanie muttered irritably to herself, willing sleep to come so that she could escape from these irrational thoughts and suppositions. He was constantly on her mind, getting under her skin to such an extent that she often had no desire to fight him.

She slept late. The soothing rocking of the boat and some rather unlikely dreams had kept her blissfully asleep until much later than usual and when she appeared Christian and Jean-Paul had already eaten and were on deck. Jean-Paul was reading and Christian was watching the shoreline through binoculars.

'You slept late today.' Christian stood and pulled out a chair for her at the table near by. 'Do they have to wake you up when one of these assignments is planned?'

'Normally I'm up early,' Stephanie assured him, her face confused at the smile he was giving her and the ready way she was accepting it.

'You can eat here,' Christian said. 'That way you will not feel you are missing things. Jean-Paul is pondering what to do with his day, expeditions being impossible.'

'I brought a few games from the house,' Stephanie admitted, silently accepting the dig at her determination to be in on everything. 'And a kite,' she added with sudden misgivings.

'A kite! Oh, wonderful! Stevie, you are the best person in the whole world,' Jean-Paul said extravagantly.

'I may well second that,' Christian murmured, 'if you do not either fall over the side or get the kite entangled in the rigging.'

'I never thought of that.' Stephanie looked crestfallen but Christian just laughed.

'So long as you watch which way the wind is blowing and act accordingly, I can see no danger. In any case,' he added sardonically, 'Michel will no doubt be honoured to climb the mast and retrieve the kite if you look at him anxiously. He was despondent that you did not join us for breakfast——'

'That's true, Stevie,' Jean-Paul interrupted gleefully. 'He asked where you were and he was *despondent*! I will get the games if I may?'

Stephanie was glad to tell him exactly where they were in her cabin. She had enough with Christian's sarcasm without Jean-Paul adding his neat little share.

'That was not a suitable conversation for a small boy,' she said primly as Jean-Paul skipped away.

'He is French,' Christian pointed out. 'Surely it is time that he recognised the difference between men and women.'

'You're being deliberately outrageous!' Stephanie snapped at him but he took her hand, hanging on to it when she would have snatched it away.

'Perhaps I am. Perhaps I am also trying to lighten the rather stifling atmosphere that has held us in its grip for some days.'

'There's no need whatever to hold my hand,' Stephanie managed, getting free and concentrating on pouring her tea.

'Again, perhaps I am wishing to make it quite clear to the men that you are under my wing,' he said softly. 'If you object, of course, I know Michel very well indeed. I can indicate to him that the coast is clear. But truly, I think you will be much safer with me. I can take care of you.'

'I can take care of myself,' Stephanie snapped, annoyed at this bantering. 'I still have my hairdrier and just remember that. You may pass this fact on to the captain.'

Christian sat back and laughed, enjoying it enormously.

'He is greatly to be trusted,' he assured her. 'You are being teased, Stephanie, and I can tell that you do not take kindly to it. I will be very serious from now on.'

He was as good as his word and later Stephanie rather wished he would continue the good-natured bantering. He ignored her completely, leaving Jean-Paul in her care and spending most of his time with Michel Arlaud. There was a lot of serious discussion and many times Christian was called to the ship's phone. There was never a time when the shoreline was left unobserved because if Christian was not on look-out some member of the crew was.

Not only did she feel left in the dark about the progress of things, she felt rather like a hired nursemaid. She played with Jean-Paul until lunchtime and later could not put off any longer the launching of the kite.

After Christian's remarks, she had been loath to get it out in case some dire mistake on her part brought problems. Now, though, she had no choice and as there was a stiff breeze Jean-Paul insisted. Stephanie admonished herself for the sheer folly of suggesting flying a kite on a boat but she was stuck with it now and if Christian thought she was foolish, then she could only agree with him.

It looked as if there would be no problem at all. The breeze was off-shore and the kite sailed out over the blue sea, even attracting the admiring attention of the crew from time to time. Stephanie had not realised until now how high the yacht stood from the water. It was indeed a very large and splendid vessel and any odd thoughts of diving over the side for a quick swim left her mind as she contemplated the sheer drop to the sea.

'Look out!'

Jean-Paul's shriek of warning came a little late. A small but boisterous gust of wind seemed to come from the sea and the kite dipped alarmingly, heading in towards the boat like some living creature on a jet stream. It was impossible to react in time and a second later Stephanie and Jean-Paul stood and glumly contemplated their bright plaything as it smashed into the rigging and wound itself fast.

'Oh, no!' Jean-Paul muttered. 'It is just what Oncle Christian warned against.' They both turned and looked guiltily around but so far their problem had not been noticed. 'I will have to tell him,' Jean-Paul stated gloomily. 'I expect he will forbid further flying now.'

'It's not far up,' Stephanie assessed, squinting up into the sun. 'Keep a look-out and I'll get it. What Uncle Christian doesn't know won't harm him.'

She kicked off her sandals and started right away but Jean-Paul was too worried to just watch.

'No, Stevie!' he pleaded urgently. 'It is too dangerous.'

'It's only like a ladder,' Stephanie assured him but he was too scared for her to stay where he was. He raced off across the deck but by this time Stephanie had rather committed herself to the task and was steadily climbing the thick ropes that made up the rigging of the yacht.

It was not at all as she had expected. In the first place, she had never had cause to climb a ladder before, in spite of her brave words to her nephew. Even if she had, a ladder would not have been swaying in the breeze, rolling with the movement of the water, and it would not be cutting into the soles of her feet as this one was.

Even before she reached the kite, she knew she was in trouble. One unwary glance down assured her of that. From the deck, it had not looked too high but from above she had to adjust her thinking. The rigging was much higher when the drop to the sea was taken into account and when she realised the height she had reached Stephanie froze.

At that moment she knew she would not be able to go either up or down. All she could do was cling on hard and try not to feel dizzy because up on the rigging the movement of the boat was greater than it had been on deck. It almost seemed to be trying to shake her off.

'Don't move!'

Christian's voice came from the deck and she looked down fearfully to see him standing below with a very anxious Jean-Paul beside him. The order had been superfluous in any case because she could not even begin to move. Her hands were clinging so tightly that the blood seemed to be leaving her fingers.

She was even more scared when she felt someone else start climbing. It caused even more swaying and her mouth felt dry with fear. She could tackle intruders much more readily than she could do this. It was a different kind of courage and right at the moment she felt she would never be safe again.

'Turn to face me.' Stephanie felt Christian's hand on her shoulder but she shook her head and bit down on her lip. Turning was quite out of the question. She rather expected a sharp command but Christian seemed to have weighed up her problem and he spoke softly, almost in her ear.

'I will not let you fall. There is only one way that I can get you down if you cannot move by yourself. Just turn slowly and it will all be over in a minute.'

It was the calm sound of his voice that gave her the courage to move; all the same, she had to shut her eyes and it was terrifying to know that Christian was right behind her, their footing very precarious.

'Now,' he said when she was facing him, 'let yourself just lean over my shoulder.'

'We'll fall.' She clung even harder but he shook his head.

'We will not fall. I have things to do; falling does not fit in with my schedule. The sooner we are down the better. The breeze is stiffening. Lean over my shoulder and we will be on the deck and quite safe in a few seconds.'

It took a lot of nerve simply to let go and place her weight on Christian and even though she had reason to know his strength she was surprised how easily he accepted her. She fastened her fingers in his belt, leaving him free to use both hands to get her down and the fact that the blood was going to her head didn't bother her at all.

'I am glad that you are wearing skimpy shorts,' Christian muttered. 'I will be able to give you a good few slaps where they are needed. I have probably left it too late, though. Your defiant habits seem to be a set part of your character.'

Even if she had been able to answer, Stephanie would have held her tongue. She was fully aware of the folly of her ways and this latest act of lunacy was her last;

she vowed that silently and solemnly. With hindsight, she could see that it would have been no problem at all either to leave the kite where it was or to let Jean-Paul wheedle round his uncle Christian.

The fact of the matter was that she had been determined to show that she was as capable as the next man. The man in question was more capable than any other man she had known and pitting herself against him was ridiculous. It was also rather childish. She intended to confess this at once but as he placed her on her feet she was too dizzy and too nauseated to say anything at all.

It seemed too that the whole crew had gathered to watch the descent and she swayed weakly as her head righted itself and the fear began to go. Christian's arm came tightly round her and he looked at one of the men, jerking his thumb towards the kite.

'Get it, Jany,' he ordered. 'You can then give it to my nephew who will put it away.' He finished with a severe look at Jean-Paul and got a very subdued nod in reply.

Christian had no further need of words. He took Stephanie to the saloon, supporting her all the way, and when she was safely sitting down on one of the long couches he handed her a brandy.

'Sip this slowly. It will bring things back to normal in no time at all.'

'I'm sorry,' Stephanie confessed, not even able to look up at him. 'It was stupid, dangerous and childish.'

'*Ma foi,*' he exclaimed mockingly, planting himself in front of her. 'I have to admit, *mademoiselle*, that when you decide to be vanquished you surpass yourself. I have never dared to put together three such crushing words to describe you.'

'You can if you like,' Stephanie murmured. 'I certainly deserve it.'

'I would never attempt to crush you,' he assured her with a laugh. He sat beside her and tilted her chin. 'Why did you climb when you are afraid of heights?'

'I'm not afraid of heights. I expected to be up there and down again with the kite before anyone even knew. I never took into consideration either the height from the sea or the swaying of the boat. I don't think I've ever been really scared before in my life.'

'Not even when you thought the men were kidnappers?'

'That was different. It was for Jean-Paul. This time I was scared for myself. I just froze.'

'I noticed.' He nodded at her brandy, urging her to drink it up. 'Lucky for you that I was at hand otherwise you may have been up there forever, travelling with us wherever we decided to sail.'

'Like the *Flying Dutchman*,' Stephanie muttered, still not sure why she was getting away with this latest escapade without some form of retaliation.

'Perhaps. I was thinking actually that you would have made a beautiful mascot,' Christian said drily. 'I would take it easy for now. Shock can sometimes come at you unexpectedly. Stay here and Jean-Paul can take care of himself. In any case, he will no doubt be very subdued. He was terrified for his beloved Stevie.'

Stephanie had no desire to move. She sank back more comfortably and after Christian left she had a hard time not to fall asleep. She was still sitting there later when Jean-Paul crept in to observe her solemnly.

'How are you, Stevie?' he enquired worriedly and she grinned at him, pulling herself together.

'Fine. I'm staying here to hide from your uncle. I also feel like a fool. The crew will be laughing at me so I'm staying right out of sight until they get about their business and forget the whole mad thing.'

'I had to get Oncle Christian,' Jean-Paul was still looking worried and Stephanie nodded in agreement.

'Thank goodness you did. I needed rescuing.'

'He is like a shining knight, is he not?' Jean-Paul demanded enthusiastically. 'Sometimes he is a little worrying but you can always know he will be there if there is trouble.'

'I know.' She had to agree and it was not just to placate her nephew. Christian always seemed to be there if trouble came and it had come several times to her since she had been on St Lucien. Her carefree and independent ways were almost gone. She knew she needed a spell of hard work to get back into her old frame of mind but this feeling of destiny was beginning to stick hard.

'Would it be all right if I were to sit on your knee?' Jean-Paul asked seriously and Stephanie looked at him sharply. It was most unusual. He too was an independent character and he had pointed out his grown status quite swiftly when Christian had attempted to carry him.

'Of course! I need a bit of comforting and a lot of courage.'

'It's not that, Stevie,' he said in a low voice, climbing up and settling himself against her shoulder. 'I want a secret talk.' He turned his head and looked up at her. 'There is something strange going on.'

Stephanie acknowledged that the time had come. It was not really a surprise. Children were intuitive and Jean-Paul was a very bright little boy.

'You mean something fishy?' she asked, trying to keep things light.

'*Comment*?' He looked at her with startled dark eyes and Stephanie ruffled his hair.

'You're as bad as your uncle,' she complained. 'He doesn't understand English sayings either. I'll try again. Do you think that something peculiar is happening?'

'I do,' he assured her, snuggling down as if seeking safety. 'Oncle Christian is not the same as usual on this trip to St Lucien. You do not really know him, Stevie. He laughs a lot and he is great fun usually but this time he is often angry and—and he is always watching me.

Now that we are here, the men are watching me too. It is all—peculiar. Fishy?'

Stephanie nodded vaguely. Now what did she do? Did she assure Jean-Paul that he was mistaken or did she try to explain? If she did that, what would Christian say? She knew too that her often heated exchanges with Christian would not have gone unnoticed. She had shouted loudly several times before she had realised the dangerous situation and Jean-Paul might well have heard enough to make him anxious.

'It's not that anything peculiar is happening,' she explained carefully. 'It's just that we're all on guard. That's why we came to the boat, so that we could be more on guard than ever.' She had Jean-Paul's undivided attention and she still hadn't quite worked out how much to tell him.

'Your uncle Christian is very rich,' she went on. 'I expect you know that?'

'Papa says he is one of the richest men in France.'

'Probably. Well, rich people are sometimes in danger because there are certain bad people who would like to get hold of the money.' She was stumbling and she knew it but Jean-Paul unexpectedly helped her out.

'There was a man in America who was kidnapped,' he said eagerly. 'Maman read it out from the paper. They wanted a large amount of money, a ransom? Do they want a ransom for Oncle Christian?'

'I think it's their plan but they haven't got him, have they? That's why we're watching.'

'Ah! I understand now. I will watch too.' He suddenly laughed, quite startling her. 'Maman and Papa talked about that when she was reading the paper. She said what a dreadful thing it would be if anyone did that to Oncle Christian. Papa said that if anyone stole Oncle Christian they would bring him back fast, just to be rid of him, because he is so hard and tough. Papa said it would be more trouble than it was worth.'

'I expect it would be,' Stephanie agreed. 'However, we're not about to let them get him, are we? That's why we're watching. We're going to get them instead.'

'I will go and help!' Jean-Paul said determinedly, climbing down and making for the outside. 'Do you have any binoculars, Stevie?'

'I'm afraid not,' she said. 'Ask one of the crew but *don't* let anyone know that you understand why they're watching. You can be an extra help. You and I will work alone.'

'Very good!' Jean-Paul exclaimed. 'It is always exciting when you are there, Stevie. Now there is an adventure.'

'True enough,' Stephanie muttered. If Christian found out there would probably be a massacre.

'I wish you always lived with us,' he added thoughtfully and Stephanie made a wry face at him.

'Believe me, I couldn't stand the pace,' she said. Whether he understood that or not she didn't know but he left to begin his secret observations and Stephanie was alone with her guilt.

A slight noise had her turning her head and she found Christian leaning in through one of the sliding windows from the deck. She could tell by his expression that he had heard at least some of the conversation and she was unnerved by the piercing blue of the eyes that studied her.

'He knows,' she confessed, thinking it better to get her word in first as his words were almost certain to be devastating.

'I heard some of your clever invention,' he admitted. 'I am not above eavesdropping when the need arises.'

'I had to tell him something because he was worried,' Stephanie said urgently. 'He was under the impression that everyone was watching him and it must have been bothering him greatly because he wanted to sit on my knee.'

'He is fortunate to be small enough,' Christian murmured sardonically. He strolled round to the door and came in. 'I agree. You had to tell him something and I was greatly impressed by your invention, a perfect lie in fact—almost the truth.'

'It wouldn't have been a good idea to let him know that he was the target,' Stephanie pointed out, beginning to get angry at what she took to be scorn.

'*D'accord*! Have I not said that I was greatly impressed? Your explanation covered everything that he is likely to find out.'

'I was floundering a bit. Jean-Paul inadvertently helped me out with his story about a ransom.'

'Yes. I heard that,' Christian assured her wryly. 'It was interesting to hear my brother's assessment of me.' Stephanie couldn't hide a smile and he shot her a glittering glance. 'I can see that you agree with him, *mademoiselle*.'

'Well, the thought has a lot going for it,' she pointed out. 'I couldn't come up with any arguments.'

'So you think I am hard and tough?'

'You've given me no reason to imagine otherwise. We haven't exactly taken to each other,' Stephanie murmured.

'I will change my ways when all this is over,' he promised drily. 'In the meantime, I will go and observe your spy. Perhaps the next rescue attempt I make will be when Jean-Paul falls overboard in his enthusiasm for watching.'

He went out and Stephanie breathed a sigh of relief. For once, he agreed with her judgement. She went to get changed. Now that things were more out in the open she had the urge to do some watching of her own and it would not be to protect the invincible Oncle Christian either. It was time that something happened, time that things came to a head, and she wanted to be right there and ready when they did.

CHAPTER EIGHT

It was almost dark when Christian had a call from the shore that had him ordering the launch out. He never mentioned it to Stephanie but on the boat it was almost impossible to take any action without it being noticed at once and she could almost feel the atmosphere in any case.

'What is it?'

She came on deck just as he was preparing to leave and he looked at her impatiently.

'Two men have been arrested. They are being held by the police and I have to go in and take a look at them. You will stay here with Jean-Paul.'

'I never expected to go with you,' Stephanie said, ignoring his tone. 'How will you know if the men are the ones...?'

'I will know,' he said grimly. 'They were not caught by chance. Did I not tell you that I have been studying their methods for some time? In any case, they will talk.'

He was anxious to be off and quite clearly not about to tell her anything else and Stephanie watched as he went down to the launch and then headed towards the cove. He had chosen to dress in black, black jeans and sweatshirt. The overall impression was quite forbidding and she wondered if he had done it deliberately. Probably not. Christian could look forbidding whenever he chose. He didn't have to dress for the part.

'Where is he going?' Jean-Paul came to stand beside her and watch the speeding launch and Stephanie decided on the truth.

'He thinks they've caught the men.'

Jean-Paul didn't answer and when she glanced at him she was quite startled to find that he looked disappointed. The adventure would soon be over and he hadn't yet had his fill of it. Stephanie made a wry face to herself. It couldn't be over soon enough for her. It was time to get back to normal and this was far from normal.

It was also time to be seeing the last of Christian because he was beginning to get through her barrier of annoyance with his odd quirks of humour and his equally odd bursts of kindness. She didn't want to be anywhere near him. He had already made too much of an impression on her mind and she would be glad to get back to London.

After Jean-Paul went to bed, she sat talking to Michel. There was still no sign of Christian and Stephanie was on edge, only vaguely listening to Michel's attempts at conversation. It was now completely dark and in spite of her determination to remain indifferent she was worried.

When they finally heard the sound of a powerful engine, Michel stood and made his way to the door.

'I will see to the launch,' he said with a glance at Stephanie's strained face. 'There is no need to worry. I have never known Christian to fail at anything.'

'The men might not have been the right ones,' she muttered but he smiled that tight smile she had become used to with Christian.

'He rarely wastes his time either. They will be the right men, *mademoiselle*, and he will have dealt with it. I will eat in my cabin tonight,' he finished. 'You will want to talk privately.'

He was gone before she could protest and Stephanie was left wondering why he had reached this conclusion. She had formed the impression that Christian told him most things in any case, much more than he told her. And Christian was nothing to her. She sincerely hoped that Michel Arlaud and the crew realised that.

All the same, she was tingling with relief when Christian walked into the cosiness of the lamplight and she admitted to herself that she had been worried all the time he was away. When she just stared at him, Christian gave a twisted smile that was almost self-mocking.

'I am back in one piece, as you see,' he murmured.

'Was it them?' Her voice was almost husky and he glanced at her keenly as he nodded.

'It was. By morning they will be on their way home to France and a nice, comfortable cell.'

'But did they confess? I mean, if you should be wrong then there's still going to be danger, and how do you know that you have them all?'

'We do not have them all,' he growled, turning to help himself to a drink. 'There are three of them left but the police know where two of them are and the last one is up to me.'

'I don't understand.' Stephanie came to stand closer, looking up at him with a puzzled frown. He was still in black and he looked most daunting, especially with that grim expression on his face.

'You are not meant to understand,' he assured her grimly, draining his glass at one go and setting it down. 'This drama has been going on for some time, long before you appeared on the scene. Jean-Paul is now safe and your part in this is over. You can go back to the glitter of the fashion world and forget all about it.'

'I'm sure I'll manage that very easily!' Stephanie was hurt by his tone and the dismissive way he was speaking to her. It had begun to matter very much how he spoke to her, in spite of what she knew about him, and it added bitterness to her voice. 'You're about to get your wishes granted at last. I'll soon be on a plane and out of your sight.'

'You are very touchy this evening, *mademoiselle*. Does your nephew know that you are about to desert him?'

'How typical!' Stephanie snapped. 'You try every which way to get rid of me and then when I'm quite ready to go you start accusing me of desertion.'

'But what else is it? We had agreed that Jean-Paul was to be taken to Paris to see his new school. We made a pact together to keep the danger from his parents. It was the sort of joint decision you have been urging since I first saw you. Now, when we are about to depart, you wish to desert us.'

'But—but you said I could go back to the glitter of the fashion world and forget all about it.'

'So you can. It is almost over. I did not say, however, that you could go back at once and I did not suggest that you forget all about *us*.'

'Will you stop this "us" business?' Stephanie ordered frustratedly. 'You've never been in this at all. My thoughts are and have always been for the safety of Jean-Paul.'

'Did you not urge me to flee when you attacked the men on the beach?' he enquired mockingly. 'Were you not afraid for my safety?' He suddenly cupped her face in his hands and looked down at her. 'And have you not been anxious all the time I have been ashore?'

'Not a bit,' Stephanie breathed unsteadily. 'I felt that Jean-Paul was safe at last. It was my first relaxing time for ages.'

'Then why were you so tight and pale when I came in just now? Why did Michel tell me that you hardly listened to his scintillating conversation?'

'He's a bore,' Stephanie averred desperately.

'You imagined that various ruffians would be waiting for me with clubs at the ready,' he insisted, ignoring her declaration about Michel. 'You were worried about me.'

'I was only worried that they would come here if...if...'

'If I turned out to be something other than invincible? You think that the crew would have simply given in?

Can you even begin to think of Michel sitting down to
let events wash over him, bore though he is?'

Having been neatly tied into knots, Stephanie turned
away but he spun her back to him and this time when
she looked up he was smiling down at her in an altogether
arrogant way.

'You were anxious about my safety,' he pronounced
firmly. 'You have become attached to your partner.'

'Pigs might fly!' Stephanie snapped but he only
laughed and caught her close.

'I have decided that in future I will simply ignore your
astonishing little statements. Obviously it is an English
code unknown to other, more civilised races. I cannot
compete.' He looked down at her flushed face and then
became more serious. 'Now,' he said firmly, 'let us be
sensible. Tomorrow we leave St Lucien and you go with
us. I have things to do and I need you. Jean-Paul needs
you too.'

'If he's no longer in danger, then ...'

'The net is not closed on all of them yet,' he pointed
out with a frown. 'The danger is very slight but I will
not be entirely satisfied until they are all under lock and
key, preferably in France. Until then I would be happier
if you were with Jean-Paul.'

'Why? You've tried your best to get rid of me.'

'Jean-Paul loves you, I know that, and you are extremely resourceful.' He shrugged, staring down at her
fixedly. 'I always know too that if I am not watching
my nephew you are—if only to get the better of me.'

'Very well,' Stephanie agreed, adding tightly, 'There's
absolutely no need to hold me. I'm not about to leap
overboard and escape.'

'That is not why I am holding you.' He went on
looking at her and Stephanie felt her face flushing under
that intent look. She made a very strong attempt to get
free. She was finding herself far too attracted to Christian
without any further complications. Getting free was not

at all easy, though. He simply pulled her closer, his blue
eyes gleaming down at her, beginning to drown her, his
intentions quite clear.

'Oh, please don't,' Stephanie begged in a desperate
voice and any lingering mockery left Christian's face.

'I need to,' he said softly. 'I cannot come back and
see you anxious and pale. I would rather see you furious
than unhappy.'

'I'll not be furious,' Stephanie said unwisely,
frighteningly aware of the strong body close to her own.
'I—I'm all right now that I can see you're safely back.'

'So you did worry.' His blue eyes darkened and he
folded her closer. 'Do not worry about me, *ma belle*. I
am more than capable of taking care of myself.'

When she just stood looking up at him he smiled that
rather twisted smile and bent his dark head to hers.

'You are certainly beautiful,' he murmured against her
face. 'I cannot think why some man has not already
captured you. Englishmen must be very slow to react.'

He turned his head and she made no attempt to escape
this time. She was already trembling with anticipation
and she just allowed him to kiss her deeply with no
thought at all of fighting. She seemed to have been
waiting all her life to feel like this.

She was locked in his arms when dinner was served
and she vaguely heard an embarrassed cough. Christian
raised his head in a very leisurely manner, signalling the
man to continue with the duty of serving the meal.

'I feel a fool!' Stephanie said crossly when the man
had gone. Christian had let her go and now, out of the
range of his magic, she was coming back to her senses
very rapidly. He shot her an amused glance and poured
wine for her.

'You do not look it. I would say that you look much
more settled than you did when I first appeared. In any
case, it is as well for the crew to know that you are not

to be looked at amorously. We still have to sail to Martinique.'

Stephanie fell silent. She had no further desire to speak to him. It was like a dash of cold water. She knew perfectly well why they were going to Martinique. Denise Pascal was there. He was going to pick her up. If he thought she was staying on board with that woman he could think again. How could he kiss her like that and then go back to his woman?

'I'll fly home from Martinique,' she stated coldly.

'We will all fly home from Martinique,' Christian corrected and his voice sounded much more cold than her own. Whatever was suddenly on his mind, it was not pleasant and she gave him an intrigued glance. Nothing was over yet. He had plans and once again she was not to be told anything about them.

They sailed for Martinique next day and in spite of everything it was an adventure. As the quiet cove was left behind, the great yacht faced the sea like something alive and Stephanie was pleased that she felt no sign of nausea at the rolling of the boat. It was wild and free, impossible to describe. The crew came alive too, leaving their constant watching of the shore to take up the duties they loved and the *Sea Queen* set out under full sail.

Stephanie stood by the rail and enjoyed it all, her dismay of the night before fading at the exhilaration of being on a large sailing vessel. After watching Christian for a while she could tell that this was something he could do equally well, with or without a captain.

He had control until they were well out to sea and he was enjoying every minute of it, no matter what his other worries were.

'Couldn't you just get there by using the engines?' she asked as he came to stand by her at the rails when he had handed over to Michel.

'Easily,' he agreed. 'It is not quite the same, however, a little more tame. I prefer sail and I thought you might be interested.'

'Oh, I am! Thank you.' She looked up at him with shining eyes. 'I've never been on anything but a ferry before.'

'What? Do they not take you on glamorous sailing expeditions when you are working?' he asked, looking down at her with amused indulgence in his mocking blue eyes.

'I work hard,' Stephanie told him firmly. 'It's not prancing about in fancy clothes. It's just hard work, sometimes uncomfortable.'

'Have you never thought of getting out of it?' Christian turned towards her, leaning back against the rail and watching her face with interest.

'It's what I do. I've been doing it for a long time now. Of course,' she added, 'one day soon, I'll be too old I expect.'

'I cannot imagine that, Stephanie,' he laughed. 'It will not matter though. You will get married and be a glamorous wife to someone.'

'I don't fancy it. I like to be free. Anyway, it won't be my only option.' She glanced up at him and then looked away quickly. He really looked superb. His dark hair was swept across his forehead by the wind and those blue eyes were narrowed against the sun as he turned away from her to look out to sea. He seemed very much at home on this boat, but then, he would look equally at home almost anywhere. He was that sort of man and she supposed it came from his self-assurance.

'If *you* married,' she mused aloud, 'you wouldn't have to spend your time guarding somebody else's child and arranging his schooling. You could have children of your own.' It was time that this business of Jean-Paul and Paris was out in the open and now seemed an ideal opportunity.

'Are you offering to marry me?' He slanted her a taunting look and she felt her face flush hotly. She had stepped into that without thought.

'No way! I'm just trying to organise your future. I'm being quite impartial.'

'Do you not mean that you are prying into my affairs?' he asked softly, turning to stare down at her in his devastating way. 'You said to yourself, He is already thirty-five; I wonder why he has not married and raised his own family? Regrettably, I cannot tell you my life story.'

'I'm sure I'd be bored. It was merely an idle thought.'

'Quite understandable,' he murmured sardonically. 'I often have idle thoughts myself. I would not mind at all having a family. The idea of beautiful, silver-haired children with large dark eyes is very tempting. The trouble would be that I would be saddled with their mother, *n'est-ce pas*? She would require constant attention and several beatings a day to keep her out of trouble. I have no time to spare for such things.'

'I was thinking of Denise,' Stephanie assured him quickly, easily following his sarcastic remarks.

'Were you? Do not trouble yourself. I think about her all the time.' He looked at her in amusement and Stephanie had a great desire to lash out at him. She was horrified at the way he could hurt her.

'No woman in her right mind would want to be attached to someone so arrogant and overwhelming as you!' she said waspishly and his lips twisted with sardonic amusement.

'*D'accord*,' he agreed as he turned away. 'But you are not exactly in your right mind, are you, *ma belle*?'

He walked off and Stephanie stared after him angrily. It was no use trying to get the better of Christian by any sort of sarcasm. He held the record for that and he used it like a dagger. She would have to leave the subject of

Jean-Paul's future to Fiona. It was unwise to interfere and might make matters worse.

Stephanie had never been to Martinique before and she looked across the sea towards it with growing interest, even though it was tinged with bitterness. Christian was coming to pick up Denise. She wondered if he planned to have his lovely family and keep Denise on at the same time. It was probably quite the usual thing in his wealthy circle.

Since the island had come into sight he had looked rather grim and he looked no better as they were called to their meal.

'If we eat now,' he said rather curtly, 'we will be quite free when we land. I have several things to do and I will organise our luggage ready for the flight. With a little luck we will be able to leave either later today or in the morning.'

'Where is this flight going to take us?' Stephanie asked quietly. She hadn't forgotten that he was insisting that she remain with Jean-Paul until this was all over.

'Paris,' he said briefly. 'It is easy enough to get to London from there.'

'I'm not exactly a millionaire,' Stephanie pointed out when Jean-Paul had been allowed to leave the table and go back to watching the sea and the busy crew. 'I doubt if I can afford to stay in Paris for long, not unless I'm willing to earn my way back to London by offering to scrub down the deck of the ferry.'

'You are with me,' Christian growled, slanting her an annoyed look. 'I will take care of all of us, in Martinique if we have to stay overnight and in Paris too. I will then take you back to London when I am satisfied that this is all over.'

'I'm big enough to travel alone,' Stephanie said sharply. 'If you're worried you can tie a label round my neck.'

'I often feel more inclined to tie a scarf over your face to stop your constant and irritating chatter,' he snapped. 'I have business in London as it happens and it has been left far too long. Jean-Paul can go with me and we can deposit you at your house or wherever you live.'

That cheered her up considerably. It meant that she would see a little more of her nephew and on her own home ground too. She looked quite pleased and Christian eyed her suspiciously.

'When we land in Martinique,' he warned her sternly, 'I want no trouble. I do not wish you to tell Denise about the capture of the men either.'

'There's little chance of that,' Stephanie snapped. 'Madame Pascal and I are not exactly on friendly terms. Jean-Paul is not likely to race up to her and tell her anything either, so set your mind at rest. I'm well aware of her delicate nature. When you get her safely back to Paris she'll be very glad, no doubt—back to civilisation.'

'Perhaps,' he muttered ironically. 'We will have to see. Meanwhile, Stephanie Caine, just remember whose side you are on.'

'I've never forgotten,' she said sweetly, tilting her head. 'I'm on Jean-Paul's side. Apart from that, I'm simply a survivor.'

'You are *barely* a survivor,' he corrected. 'Remember that without me you would still be clinging to the rigging in a most extraordinary manner.'

He nodded at her with taunting politeness and walked out on to the deck and Stephanie glared after him. In about half an hour she would have to watch him being reunited with his mistress. If Denise annoyed her she might just tell the woman how nice it had been when Christian had kissed her. She shut that thought off swiftly. It had been more than nice and it was still lingering in her mind. The thought of it brought a shiver to her skin and she had the decided feeling that he had not even been trying hard. If he really turned his attention on her she would not be a survivor at all.

Just outside the superb harbour, the *Sea Queen* dropped anchor and Christian came to give Stephanie the latest news.

'There is no flight to Paris today. We would be very rushed to catch the last one and it is simply easier to wait until tomorrow. We will remain on the boat and go in tomorrow morning.'

Stephanie just nodded, hiding her disappointment at not being about to wander around the bustling port she could see.

'There will be other times to see Martinique,' he said quietly, watching her expression. 'Remember that the danger is not entirely over and here you are safe. I have to go ashore but I will be back. Stay with Jean-Paul. I need you here.'

'Of course.' She turned away but he muttered something in exasperation and grasped her arm, swinging her back to face him.

'You can be most annoying,' he told her in a frustrated voice. 'I have never met anyone like you before in my life. You are a grown woman, doing a demanding job, showing a great deal of courage when it is needed and yet you manage to make me feel like a villain just because I do not choose to take you with me to see Martinique, hold your hand and buy you a balloon.'

'If you feel like a villain it has nothing to do with me,' Stephanie assured him crossly, pulling to get away and not succeeding. 'I don't know what gives you the idea that I want to go anyway. I can manage quite well without seeing your dramatic reunion with Madame Pascal.'

'If I tell you that you sound jealous you will, no doubt, fly into a rage and shout,' he muttered angrily. 'There are many things that you do not know. I am following a plan and nothing is about to stop me, not even your disappointed expression.' He let her arm go, almost

flinging it away. 'Think whatever you like but stay here
and watch Jean-Paul. You can be assured that I will be
back before nightfall. I would not dare leave you after
dark. You would probably construct a canoe and paddle
in unseen.'

He stormed out and Stephanie stared after him in some
exasperation. She couldn't see at all why he was so annoyed; she hadn't asked for one thing, she had even
hidden her disappointment. She would much rather sleep
on board than in some hotel and she could do without
even one glance at Denise Pascal.

Christian had an uncanny way of picking up on her
wandering thoughts. She would have liked to see something of the port but most of all she had wanted to go
with him, and as to how she felt about Denise—well,
she *was* jealous and it was useless to deny it.

It seemed to be exceptionally quiet after Christian had
gone. He was not back for dinner and after eating alone
Stephanie and Jean-Paul sat on the deck and watched
the lights of the port until it became late. After that,
Stephanie watched by herself, her mind wandering re-
luctantly to Christian and Denise. He would be dining
with her, maybe staying so late because he couldn't tear
himself away. He had promised to be back before it was
dark but obviously he couldn't bear to leave.

She went to bed feeling quite miserable but she was
very uneasy too and she was still awake when she heard
the launch cruise quietly up to the boat and stop. Then
there was nothing, no sound at all, and Stephanie sat
up, her ears straining to listen. Perhaps it was not
Christian. Perhaps they were back to danger. He had
said that two had not been caught and that one other
was up to him. How could he have left knowing that?
How could he just abandon them?

When she heard nothing more she got quietly out of
bed. The fact that there were Christian's men on board
meant nothing. She still only felt safe if Christian was

there. Jean-Paul was still her concern too and he was just as much alone in his bed here as he had been at the house.

He was sleeping peacefully when she went to look in on him but there seemed to be an extra silence to the boat that made her very anxious. She went on deck quietly, stopping with sudden shock as she saw someone standing looking out to sea. The figure was in a deep patch of shadow, hidden from the moonlight and although it might have been one of the crew Stephanie was now fully alert.

She crept forward, not really knowing what she would do if it turned out to be an intruder, but before she could take any action a voice she knew only too well spoke darkly.

'Spare me. I am unarmed.'

Christian stepped from the shadows, standing in the brilliant moonlight and looking at her intently.

'Why are you standing there like a burglar?' she demanded crossly, angry that she had been frightened and more angry still that he had been with Denise. 'I had no idea who it was. And why did you come back and then behave so silently?'

'I doubt if burglars waste their time watching the moonlight on the water,' he surmised drily. 'As to behaving silently, what would you have had me do, arouse the whole crew and waken everyone else? I thought I was being considerate.' He regarded her sardonically and she glared at him, frustrated by his wry amusement.

'You should have been back before dark as you promised!' Stephanie countered angrily, keeping her voice low. 'They're not all caught yet.'

'They are as good as caught,' he assured her in a suddenly tight voice, turning away to look at the sea. 'As to being back earlier, it was impossible. I knew things were safe here.'

'Yes, you knew I'd be sitting on guard while you— while you...'

'While I what?' he snapped, spinning to face her. 'You have not the faintest idea about my activities on shore.'

'I only need an imagination. I've managed well without a crystal ball. You're quite prepared to leave Jean-Paul at risk when you go to that woman!'

'Can you never watch that biting tongue?' he grated, grasping her by the shoulders and giving her a shake. 'You pointed out recently that I do not know you. You do not know me either, *mademoiselle*. If you knew me a little better you would not be constantly looking for selfish motives in everything I do!'

'I don't care what you do!' She flung herself away to walk off but he caught her hand before she could take more than two steps.

'Oh, Stephanie, come here! *Mon Dieu*, you drive me mad. Why are you on deck, undressed as usual? Why do you constantly pry into my affairs and my motives and then declare that you are not interested in anything I do?'

'Because I'm not.' She couldn't move away without a struggle but she refused to look at him and his fingers began to move subtly over her hand, massaging the soft skin almost absent-mindedly.

'Don't lie, *petite*. We are very interested in each other and you know it,' he murmured huskily. 'You fight me because you fear any kind of surrender and I keep you under whatever control I am able because I dare not let you get too close.'

'I—I don't understand...' she began and he looked down at her disturbingly, taking her other hand and drawing her forward towards him.

'You understand,' he said softly. 'You have always understood. That is why you fight so ferociously, because to give in to me would be surrendering your soul. Admit it, Stephanie.'

'It's not true,' Stephanie said wildly and he drew her further towards him, pulling her arms around his waist as his hands clasped her head and held it up to his.

'It is true. I snap at you for the very same reason. I have no right to want you.'

'You—you don't. You dislike me...and—and Denise...'

Stephanie felt panic growing. Her breasts were suddenly painful, tight against the thinness of her robe, and she was desperate that Christian shouldn't know the effect he was having on her. It was much too late, though, and she was much too close to him. He moved almost imperceptibly and the hard muscles of his chest pressed against the taut fullness of her breasts.

She gasped, unable to conceal the feelings that shot through her, and he looked down in the moonlight, seeing her arousal all too well. When their eyes met she couldn't look away at all.

'Do you still say it is untrue? You want me almost as dangerously as I want you.' His voice had darkened and he held her eyes with his. 'I did warn you that as a silky adversary you would be too much for my self-control,' he murmured and before she could close her parted lips his mouth covered hers.

She resisted him as hard as she could, moving her body in agitation, but it only made her more aware of him, more aware of her own needs, and his grip on her simply tightened. She was already too close to him for any resistance to be effective and he released her head, closing his arms around her and moving closer with a satisfied sigh.

'Please...' she begged and his hold on her became gentle at once, his hands sliding down her body to her hips. It stilled her resistance and his mouth teased at hers, quietly and gently insistent until her lips parted and his own lips opened to accommodate hers.

It was different then and feelings flared inside her until she wanted to press against him, feel his hands all over her. When he drew her against him completely she felt the urgent stirring of his body, the first time she had ever felt it with any man. She could feel a hunger inside him, the muscular power of his body held back only by his iron will.

He wanted to devour her and she had an overwhelming urge inside her to yield against him and let it all happen but she knew it was madness, sexual arousal that had come from out of nowhere. Whatever her own desires she could not forget Denise. She had to get away from him fast and she looked up in a panic-stricken way to find blue eyes blazing down at her.

'Let me go,' she whispered. 'I—I hate you and—and...'

'Don't,' he begged softly. 'Don't, Stephanie, *chérie*.' He rubbed his cheek against hers with a sort of controlled tenderness that only added to her confusion and when her resistance suddenly crumbled he spread his opened palms around her hips, stroking subtly and rhythmically, moving the silk of her skimpy clothing against her skin.

He gave a low groan, deep in his throat, and when his head bent to hers again he was gentle, his tongue teasing at her lips until she sighed and opened her mouth wide again, allowing him to deepen the kiss to passion. She had never had feelings like the ones she had then. She wanted to mould herself tightly to him and her hands found their way into his thick, dark hair as she gave herself up to the heat that flooded her limbs.

Like someone in a dream she let him lead and willingly followed. She was hardly aware that his hands had moved until she felt the arousing pressure of his fingertips against her breasts and his name left her lips in a sobbing breath as molten feeling curled in her stomach and moved into her legs.

'No, Christian!'

'Why?' he asked thickly. 'Why no? You have never been afraid of me. Are you afraid now because I want to take you to my cabin and sleep with you, feel you close to me in the night?'

The softly spoken words sent a shaft of feeling through her that made her legs more weak than ever and she knew she had to stop this now or it would be too late. She admitted that she wanted to go with him, that each time he had kissed her she had wanted to continue, even when he had kissed her harshly. It was something she had resolutely pushed to the very back of her mind but now she felt the same hunger that he was feeling and she had almost no defence.

'I—I'm not afraid of you,' she managed shakily, making herself draw back from the sensual dream he had stirred. 'I'm just disgusted. Do you want any woman who happens to be there at the time? Does Denise know about your weakness?'

He stiffened as if she had slapped his face and the blue eyes that had blazed down at her in passion now blazed with anger.

'I have few weaknesses, *mademoiselle*,' he grated harshly, 'and women are not one of them. In any case, you are not a woman, are you? The moment I touch you you behave like a frightened girl and always you use anger to protect yourself. You need not protect yourself from me. Go to bed before we say anything else to each other. There is tomorrow and for Jean-Paul's sake we must be at least civilised.'

Stephanie turned away, almost in tears. She felt guilty, shaken and utterly forlorn, unaware that her whole body showed the state of her mind.

'Stephanie!' His hand closed convulsively on her shoulder and she stopped, keeping her face averted almost desperately. 'I'm sorry,' he said softly. She never moved and his hand relaxed to gentleness. He gave a sigh that was not at all steady before he said, 'I never meant to hurt you, to upset you. I could not hurt you— ever. There is a need in me to protect you as much as I wish to protect Jean-Paul. You just do not understand.'

'It's all right,' Stephanie whispered, tears starting to her eyes. 'I expect I'm provocative, pitting my puny strength against yours most of the time. In any case, you didn't exactly surprise me. You've behaved like an aggressive male right from the first. I imagine this evening was just another line of attack.'

She heard his savage intake of breath and his hand left her shoulder abruptly. She had hit out at him bitterly and the words had struck home only too well. He never spoke as she made her escape while she could. It would not do for him to see her cry. Crying was not part of her image. She held it back until she was safely locked in her room and even then she did her sobbing into the thickness of the pillow.

CHAPTER NINE

IT WAS a very grim party that left the *Sea Queen* next morning and took the launch to Martinique's capital of Fort-de-France and its busy harbour. Christian had never spoken at all and Jean-Paul, after watching them both with bright-eyed intelligence, lapsed into silence too. It was impossible to put on a cheerful face, even for his sake, although Stephanie tried.

This morning she was pale under her tan and after one glance at Christian she knew he would not forgive her for the words she had spoken last night. She told herself frantically that she did not care at all but even as she thought it she knew she lied to herself. She cared a great deal. She was drawn to Christian, wanted to look at him all the time, wanted his gentle indulgence and his arms around her. There was this feeling of fate, as if it had all been decided a long time ago. Right now she could not imagine having any sort of relationship with any man other than Christian.

She compressed her lips and carefully looked away from him. She dared not even meet his cold blue glance and it would be good when she was free to go back to her own life. She would get over it as soon as she couldn't see him again. She knew already that she could not stay in Paris at all, could not share the duty of looking after Jean-Paul. Denise would be there, constantly under her nose, constantly with Christian, and she couldn't face that even once.

Stephanie was obliged to face it, though, when they landed. Christian had done a lot of organising and if she had still been inclined to wander around the port she would have been disappointed again. A car was waiting for them as they landed and their luggage was swiftly transferred to the boot as they were ordered to get in.

'Are we going to stay here at a hotel, Oncle Christian?' Jean-Paul ventured when Stephanie said nothing at all.

'We are not,' Christian stated grimly. 'Our arrival has been timed so that we can leave almost immediately. We are going straight to the airport. There is a plane for France right now and we will be on it.' He looked down at his nephew and smiled rather tightly. 'We are going home, *mon ami*.'

Jean-Paul looked a little scared as far as Stephanie could see. France was not his home at all but no doubt Christian would see to it that it became his home. At the moment, Jean-Paul didn't even have his parents and Stephanie felt another rush of guilt when she realised that in her own misery she was ignoring a small boy's anxieties.

'Paris is wonderful,' she assured him quickly. 'It's an exciting place. You'll love it.'

'There are lots of people there to steal Oncle Christian,' he mused worriedly and before Christian could intervene Stephanie spoke firmly.

'They're all captured,' she said decisively.

'All of them?' He looked greatly relieved and Stephanie didn't much care about lying.

'Everyone in the bag,' she assured him.

'So we will be free to go all over, Stevie? We can have expeditions in Paris?' He had brightened up at once but Stephanie couldn't let him have false hopes.

'You can have expeditions with Uncle Christian,' she said quietly. 'I'll have to go home.'

'You are leaving us, Stevie?' Jean-Paul's question tore at her heart because it was so close to the truth. It was not just a little boy she was leaving, it was Christian too, and his stiff silence told her he had noted the innocent question very well indeed.

'I work, Jean-Paul,' she pointed out gently. 'In my business you can't afford much time off or your face is forgotten.'

'How can it be forgotten?' Jean-Paul asked indignantly. 'It is the most beautiful face in the whole world. I think so and Papa thinks so, even Maman agrees. It is the most beautiful face in the world, is it not, Oncle Christian?' he demanded, turning to look at his uncle who sat grimly beside them in the car.

Christian didn't have much choice. He turned and smiled down at Jean-Paul and then his eyes ran slowly over Stephanie's strained face. It was an inspection she would have gladly avoided. His eyes lingered over her skin and then rested on her soft lips that were suddenly trembling.

'Yes,' Christian murmured tensely. 'It is the most beautiful face in the world. We are all agreed on that.'

'You see?' Jean-Paul turned to her eagerly. 'They will not forget you, Stevie. You can safely come to Paris.'

Safely! She would never be safe close to Christian but she managed a smile.

'One day soon,' she promised. 'I have a job. I work for a living and I can't just ignore the fact.'

To her relief he dropped the subject but she thought it was more that they had stopped at the airport than that he was prepared to give ground. There was a lot of Christian in Jean-Paul, the same determination to have things sorted out to his satisfaction. Christian got out of the car and as they prepared to follow Jean-Paul suddenly stopped dead, bumping into Stephanie.

'She is here,' he hissed quietly, for her ears alone. 'She is right here, waiting for us. Look, Stevie! It is Madame Pascal. She is going to Paris with us. You cannot leave me when we get there. If that lady stays with Oncle Christian, I will run away.'

Stephanie couldn't think of anything to say because she knew how he felt. When Denise came forward to meet them she wanted to turn away but her eyes seemed to be unable to leave them.

'Oh, Christian!' Denise sighed. 'It seems so long since last night.'

Stephanie closed her eyes but even so she was not quick enough and couldn't miss seeing the way that Christian kissed her and held her. She felt sick inside, no longer outraged. All she wanted to do was creep away and never be seen again.

'Stevie?' Jean-Paul pleaded and she took a very deep breath, summoning up an altogether different kind of courage.

'Count on me,' she whispered. 'If she stays then I'll stay too. I'll see you through the bad times. With a bit of luck, somebody will kidnap her.'

Jean-Paul giggled with relief and then turned to her, hugging her as close as he could.

'I love you, Stevie,' he pronounced clearly. Christian was just coming up and his face tightened at the words. He no doubt thought she was once again pushing herself in where she was not wanted.

'Our flight is called,' he said stiffly. 'Come along, Jean-Paul I will get you settled.'

'I intend to go with Stevie,' Jean-Paul said stubbornly, setting his lips tightly and meeting the brilliant blue eyes with a certain amount of rebellion on his face. 'I shall sit with her all the way there.'

'I do not doubt it,' Christian answered grimly. 'If you have further plans I'm sure you will let me know.' He signalled them forward and Jean-Paul slid his hand in Stephanie's. Right now he was more like Christian than Fiona. There had been no wheedling, no cajoling, just the firmly stated intention.

Stephanie saw Christian's grim face and raised eyebrows. He probably thought she had arranged it and left

it to Jean-Paul to speak. Unless she was mistaken, he
was about to find out that he had a handful with his
nephew and as she looked at Denise clinging to
Christian's arm she felt glad about it. Let him cope.
Anyway, Fiona would be back before too long and he
would have two handfuls then if he tried his domineering ways with her. She would weep, moan and
scream. It would be a laugh to see. If he thought *she*
drove him mad, wait until he had some time with Fiona.

Their seats were opposite each other and Stephanie let
Jean-Paul have the window seat, rather dismayed when
she found that this left her sitting just across the aisle
from Christian. Not that he even acknowledged her
presence. He was utterly taken up with Denise, who sat
with her arm entwined with his. She looked particularly
pleased with herself this morning and Stephanie turned
away, determined not to look again. No doubt Denise
was looking forward to Paris and being able to be with
Christian all the time. Stephanie closed her eyes and bit
her lip hard. She had just promised Jean-Paul that she
would stay if that woman stayed with Christian, but how
could she?

In the first place she would not be able to bear it,
seeing him with someone else all the time. In the second
place, he had never suggested today that she should stay.
She could hardly insist. Once again she had got herself
into a fix and right at that moment she couldn't see a
way out of it. Her face went even more tense.

'You are all right?' Stephanie opened her eyes to find
Christian leaning across, his eyes intently on her face.

'Yes, thank you,' she said quietly and coldly. 'I'm not
afraid of flying; I do a lot of it in my job.'

'You are pale,' he insisted and she wished he would
leave her alone, get back to his mistress and ignore her
so that she could try to forget him just for a minute.

'I'm tired,' she told him shortly. 'I'll sleep for most
of the journey.'

'As you wish, *mademoiselle*,' he said with equal coldness. 'You may be assured that I will take care of my nephew.'

'Or Madame Pascal will?' Stephanie could have choked as she let the bitter words escape from her mouth but it was too late.

'As you pointed out long ago,' he murmured icily, 'she is not exactly motherly. It does not matter, however. She has other attributes.'

Stephanie turned her head, her face going paler still, and he did not attempt to speak to her again. Before too long, Jean-Paul's eyes began to close and when she had him comfortable Stephanie willed herself to sleep. She had slept very little during the night; misery and a deep, heated longing had kept her awake and now she let her seat back to be level with Jean-Paul's and slept. It was, after all, the only escape she had.

It was a relief to know that they were landing when they reached Paris. Stephanie had managed to sleep for some of the time but she could not in any way escape from Christian. Nor could she fail to hear Denise's voice as she spoke to him. It actually hurt to hear her speaking so seductively and to hear Christian's frequent soft laughter.

By the time they landed Stephanie felt that she would have to escape no matter what happened and she was quite prepared for a scene as far as Jean-Paul was concerned. She had made her mind up. She would offer to have him with her in London and she would tell Christian outright that Jean-Paul would not countenance staying anywhere near that woman.

She did not have the chance to say anything at all. There was the bustle of disembarking, the steady movement towards Passport Control and then they were ready to collect their luggage. Stephanie had no intention of handing her luggage over to Christian and she was very much on edge as they came out to get it.

'I'll take care of my own things,' she said quickly as Christian reached to get them. He turned on her immediately.

'I told you—no trouble!' he grated in a low, furious voice. 'I have things to see to, things that cannot wait.'

'I can't wait either,' Stephanie said sharply. 'I'm not even leaving the airport. When the flight to London leaves, I'll be on it.'

Christian went very still, menacingly so, his eyes narrowed and brilliantly angry but Stephanie couldn't stop. She was miserable, hurt. Even in this situation his glance was not solely confined to her—he looked frequently at Denise, who stood a short way off. He seemed to be afraid he would lose sight of her and it made Stephanie more bitter still. There was not much chance of Denise leaving him.

'I'm taking Jean-Paul with me,' she stated determinedly and then she had his complete attention.

'*Ma fois*, you are not!' He grasped her arm but she pulled away angrily.

'You think he'll want to stay with you and that—that woman? He's already told me that he'll run away. You're as good as kidnapping him yourself. Fiona and Thierry don't want Jean-Paul in Paris with you. They don't want their son taken over like some business venture. They don't want him brought up in your image.'

'Then they may tell me themselves,' Christian said icily. 'In the meantime, he stays with me. Attempt to take him with you, *mademoiselle*, and I will have you arrested!'

It was said so vehemently, so coldly that it silenced Stephanie completely. She had not one doubt that he meant it and who would listen to her if it happened? Christian, after all, had more rights than she had herself, especially here in France.

'As you are determined to be independent,' Christian rasped when he saw that she was unable to answer, 'gather your luggage and come to say your goodbyes to your nephew. Once again, he is standing forlornly watching us quarrel. I may be hard as you imagine, *mademoiselle*, but I do not give him cause to grieve.'

He turned away, walking to Jean-Paul, who looked on the very edge of tears, and taking his hand firmly. He then collected Denise, who smiled up at him sympathetically. She had seen yet another quarrel and she shook her head mournfully and slid her hand into Christian's.

Stephanie saw his hand tighten and she admitted defeat. All she could do was follow them and she did, her luggage on a trolley, her heart pounding with misery. She couldn't believe it was over, that she would never see Christian again.

When she looked up, several policemen were walking steadily towards them and after one quite uninterested glance Stephanie looked back quickly. Their eyes were fixed on her and there was little doubt that they were making their way forward to speak to her. Her heart almost stopped as so many things ran through her mind. Could Christian have anticipated her reaction to being in Paris? Could he have suspected that she would try to take Jean-Paul? Could it be something to do with Fiona? Was she worse?

She stood absolutely still. Even Jean-Paul was watching with a worried look on his face and she suddenly knew that for some reason or other they were going to arrest her.

Christian was watching too, his hand protectively on Denise's arm and a look of satisfaction on his face. As the policemen came up to Stephanie she could not say a word and Christian merely watched coldly.

'*Madame.*' The leading policeman looked severely at Stephanie but before he could continue Christian was there, bringing Denise with him.

'I am Christian Durand,' he told them quietly.

'*Oui*, Monsieur Durand. We recognised you. That is how we know...'

'You do not know,' Christian stated grimly. 'You are looking in the wrong direction. *This* is Madame Pascal.'

The hand that had been holding Denise so considerately now tightened to steel and he moved her forward until she was facing the police.

'Christian? What is this?' Denise gave a small laugh of confusion but she received no answering smile from Christian.

'This, Denise, is the end of the line,' he assured her coldly. 'It was amusing but it is over.'

'Denise Pascal, you are under arrest.' The police took over and Christian let go of her arm as she was instantly held in a similar manner by one of the policemen.

'Christian? Is this one of your peculiar jokes?' she asked almost hysterically. 'You are tired of me so you are having me arrested? I knew you were powerful but I did not know you were mad. You are now interested in this English girl?'

'I am interested in no one,' Christian stated flatly. 'Mademoiselle Caine had one function only—to help me to catch you. It has never been a joke; if it had been, it would have been a most distasteful one. I have you safely back in France, *madame*, and that is exactly where I meant you to be. From now on you are not my responsibility. I understand that the law takes a very grim view of threats to kidnap.'

'You—you must really be out of your mind!' At first she was angry, prepared to bluster but after one look at Christian's icy face she crumbled. 'After everything that has happened between us——' she began tearfully, but Christian turned away impatiently.

'You may remember it when you are in prison,' he rasped. 'Your companions will be there also. You will have much to discuss at the trial.'

'You have no proof!' Denise spat out viciously but he smiled that cool smile that Stephanie had seen so often.

'I have been gathering proof for a very long time,' he assured her, 'long before you insinuated yourself into my life. I was expecting you, *madame*, or someone very much like you. All I had to do was keep you close until we had the others. Now we have all of you.'

Stephanie watched with an almost open mouth as Denise struggled violently, all her sophistication gone.

'She is one of them?' Jean-Paul asked in astonishment as she was forcibly led away. 'Madame Pascal was going to kidnap you, Oncle Christian?'

'Well, she knew that she would need help,' Christian said with mocking amusement, looking down into his nephew's startled eyes. 'I do not imagine that she felt capable of bundling me into a bag all by herself.'

'I never liked her. It just goes to show,' Jean-Paul said vehemently. 'Stevie did not like her either.' He suddenly looked up and waved vigorously. 'There is André,' he said happily.

Stephanie went to stop him but he was already running towards a stocky Frenchman who was beaming at him.

'André is my chauffeur,' Christian said tersely. 'Jean-Paul is safe. Do not attempt to stop him or influence him in any way. You can only bring unhappiness and I will not allow it.'

He looked down at her coldly and Stephanie just stared back at him, his harsh words washing over her.

'You knew?' she asked, returning to the events that had stunned her.

'I knew.'

'You knew right from the first.'

'All the time, *mademoiselle*.' He turned away, looking round impatiently, signalling for a porter.

'I'm going back to London, anyway,' Stephanie said quietly. 'Now that she's not going to be there to upset Jean-Paul . . .'

'She has never been allowed to upset Jean-Paul,' Christian said in a chilly voice. 'If you think back carefully, *mademoiselle*, you will find that she had very little to do with him. He may imagine that I was about to be kidnapped but it never slipped my mind even once that Jean-Paul was in danger. I rarely took my eyes from Denise. You have already said that you are going back to London. Do not let me detain you. You have made your opinion of me very plain on many occasions. You have made it particularly plain since we landed in Paris. There is a flight to London now and I suggest that you get it. I will be busy taking over my nephew's life from now on.'

'I didn't know——' Stephanie began miserably, but he cut in on her with the old ruthless manner he had had when they first met.

'No, you did not know but you judged. Your sister too—judged because you were speaking her words, not Thierry's. It is a thread that runs through your family quite obviously. I have always pitied my brother. He married too young and he married unwisely. He seems to be about to pay for that for the rest of his life. It is time for intervention.'

'What are you going to do?' Stephanie whispered.

'No doubt you will hear it all from your sister when you are commiserating with her about the French ways of Frenchmen,' Christian grated. 'Meanwhile, Mademoiselle Caine, your flight is due. I suggest that you rush back to the calm safety of England.'

Jean-Paul came running back and Stephanie crouched down beside him, fighting off tears.

'I'm going home, Jean-Paul,' she said softly, hugging him when his eyes too clouded over. 'You'll see me soon, don't worry. When your mother and father get back they'll bring you to see me. Maybe they'll even let you stay with me for a while and then we'll have some good expeditions in London.'

'I would rather have you now, Stevie,' he confessed tearfully but she smiled at him and shook her head.

'You have Uncle Christian,' she reminded him. 'There's no danger now and that awful woman has gone. You'll be happy.'

'There is a lot to do,' Christian intervened, taking Jean-Paul's arm and detaching him from Stephanie. 'You must get to know Paris really well and from now on you will speak only in French. It will prepare you for school.'

'I wonder when Papa and Maman will arrive?' Jean-Paul mused unhappily, glancing at Stephanie and she had to put on a brave face.

'Any time now. So you see, we'll all be together in no time at all.'

'And Oncle Christian too?' Jean-Paul asked hopefully.

'André may need some help with the luggage,' Christian pointed out diplomatically. 'Kiss your aunt goodbye and see what you can do.'

It had the effect of stiffening Jean-Paul's rather wilting appearance and after a great hug and kiss he once again ran to Christian's chauffeur.

'Thank you,' Stephanie whispered, looking down at the floor. 'If he had cried I don't think I could have...'

'He will not cry. I will see to that. Your flight is being called,' he coolly. 'I suggest that you go before he can once again capture you.'

'Don't try to make me feel guilty,' Stephanie said bitterly.

'Am I doing that? You have promised him that you will see him, that you will all be together. Why should you feel guilty, *mademoiselle*? Do not worry, I will not attempt to be there to join the happy reunion.'

She was feeling guilty all the same and not for Jean-Paul. She had misjudged Christian in so many things. She had probably misjudged him in everything but it was too late now.

'I can understand why you had to—to play up to her,' she said dully and he looked at her with cool contempt.

'Can you?' he asked cynically. 'It was a small enough sacrifice to make in order to get her under lock and key. In any case, it means very little to a man; sometimes it means absolutely nothing at all. It is merely mechanical.'

'Don't you mean—animal?' Stephanie corrected, her face going white. She turned away to the desk, not even doing more than wave to Jean-Paul. She had to get out of here fast. Already she could feel tears stinging at her eyes. It would have meant nothing to Christian if she had surrendered either.

She got her ticket almost blindly, not hearing a thing that was said to her, making her way unsteadily to the wrong gate.

'Not here!' Christian's hand came to her arm and he turned her to the correct gate. Tears were streaming down her face unchecked, running into her mouth, down to her neck and he pulled her to a halt as she was about to go through the barrier.

'Stephanie!' he muttered angrily. 'What am I going to do about you?'

'Nothing,' she choked, wrenching herself free. 'I'm not your problem any longer and I never will be because I'll never see you again. Goodbye.'

She walked away and he did nothing to stop her. She never looked round either. It was over, quite over. Her dream island was ruined because she would never go back there without seeing Christian on every stretch of sand, on every blue wave. She would hear his voice on the wind and see his brilliant eyes in the bright sky. She would never visit St Lucien again, no matter what problems Fiona invented.

During the next couple of weeks Stephanie had one brief letter from Jean-Paul. It was full of enthusiastic accounts of his excursions with Uncle Christian and it was very obvious that he had settled well enough without her. Christian would have seen to that.

She did not think this with any kind of bitterness; Christian loved Jean-Paul and he knew that he would miss her if he had time on his hands. How Christian was able to carry on with his work and still go out with this regularity, taking Jean-Paul sightseeing, she did not know.

Without realising it her mind began to dream of Christian with his own children, children with silvery hair and dark eyes, he had said. His taunting voice came back to her and she pulled herself up sharply. She could not afford to dream, especially when it was about things he had merely been goading her with.

She had given up any thought of trying to stop him keeping Jean-Paul. It was Fiona's job and Thierry's. She wasn't even sure if she believed it now. It might just have been one of Fiona's plots.

'You look terrible!' Debra Swift, her agent, said in a horrified voice when she went along to the office to check out her jobs.

'Thank you,' Stephanie murmured drily. 'Nothing like the truth to boost the old ego.'

'Oh, stop it!' Debra muttered impatiently. 'You know perfectly well how you look, you're professional. The face is the same but I warn you, it's getting a bit thin, that's aging, my pet! You've almost lost that glorious tan too. You're going to have to go on the sunbed.'

'I thought the pale look was in?' Stephanie enquired, glancing at herself, not really interested in the reflection that stared back with over-large eyes.

'Not for you. In any case, you're neither one thing nor the other. Your tan is going too fast and it's because you're pale underneath it. Not ill, are you?' Debra suddenly enquired suspiciously.

'Never better,' Stephanie lied cheerfully.

'Pregnant?'

'Watch it!' Stephanie warned and Debra shrugged unconcernedly.

'Well, you never know. I just think you're keeping something back from me.'

'You're my agent, not my psychiatrist,' Stephanie pointed out. 'Let's get to the jobs, if any.'

'Plenty,' Debra said with satisfaction. 'Too many. A few more than you can take on, I think. I'll get it all worked out and give you a schedule but you're going to be run off your feet after next week so you'd better get some rest, some sleep—or something.'

Or something, Stephanie mused as she stepped back out into the busy street. She wasn't getting either rest or sleep. She just felt haunted. She even imagined that she saw Christian in every passing car, in every shop window. He was in Paris and she had better get him out of her mind for good. If he had cared about her he would have come.

She hadn't been in more than ten minutes when Fiona and Thierry arrived and she simply fell into Fiona's arms. This was her sister. She was annoying, bossy, cunning and she manipulated people but Fiona loved her. She never doubted that.

'I'm alive, well and back in London,' Fiona assured her with a laugh as she finally extricated herself from Stephanie's hugs. 'I have a slight limp but that will go. How about some tea? Thierry and I are just fading away.'

'Oh, I'm sorry,' Stephanie murmured contritely, looking up at Thierry who was watching her with some concern. She gave him a kiss on his cheek and she shied off quickly when he gathered her close and held for a minute. It felt as if he was weighing her and she scuttled off to the kitchen before he could say anything at all.

She was thankful that he didn't look like Christian. That would have been too much to bear. She brought the tea in, her smile securely in place, and Fiona looked at her steadily when she had taken a good long drink.

'We have to thank you,' she said sincerely. 'We've been to Paris and Christian told us everything. I know it must have taken a lot of courage to do the things you did, Stephanie, and I know it must have been a hard decision to keep it from us.'

'We will never place you in such a position again,' Thierry said firmly. 'You could have been hurt.'

'Well, I wasn't,' Stephanie assured him cheerfully. She was but it was not the sort of hurt that Thierry meant. 'Looking back, it was quite an adventure.'

'We're grateful that Jean-Paul never knew that he was in danger,' Thierry said. 'Christian told us about your quick invention when Jean-Paul was worried. You must be something of an actress.'

'Lying is easy when you get the hang of it,' Stephanie informed them with a grin. It was hard to smile, hard to keep the sparkle in her eyes. Why did they have to keep mentioning Christian?

'He's moving us to Paris,' Fiona said, almost as if she could hear his name in Stephanie's mind. 'He says we shouldn't be separated from Jean-Paul and I must say, it's a relief.'

It was a shock to Stephanie and she was hard pressed to keep her cheerful looks intact. Did it mean that Christian had taken note of the harsh words she had thrown at him in Paris, or had he intended to do that all the time? She remembered what he had said about Thierry marrying unwisely, about his decision to intervene, and she looked at Fiona worriedly.

'Did you bring Jean-Paul with you now?' Normally she would have been overjoyed. She would have spent every spare minute in Paris to be with her nephew and her sister but now, of course, she could not. There was Christian and he was about to do something, she was sure of that.

'He's with Christian,' Thierry said. 'We go back to Paris tonight. We are only here to see you, *ma chère*. In two days we go to St Lucien to wind up our affairs and Jean-Paul goes with us. We'll be settled in Paris in time for him to start at his new school.'

Stephanie looked at them closely. There was something different about Fiona and about Thierry too. He was more firm, more decisive and Fiona was certainly taking a back seat. She didn't know if they had both received a strict lecture from Christian or if the accident had changed Thierry's way of looking at things. He was now quite obviously more dominant.

'You're too thin!' Fiona suddenly declared, giving Stephanie an older-sister look. 'What happened to you? Are you ill?'

'I'm perfectly all right,' Stephanie said quickly. 'I've got loads of work lined up,' she added, getting off the subject of her appearance as fast as possible. 'There's a new perfume; they want the face for that. And, believe it or not, Weston's want me.'

'The jewellers?' Fiona was instantly intrigued and Stephanie felt on safe ground, her sister's mind diverted.

'Yes. They want the hands and arms. I'm waiting to hear from Debra about the rest of me. Somebody is sure to want the whole works.'

When Fiona went to powder her nose, Stephanie looked warily at her brother-in-law. He was still watching her closely and she could see that he had not been taken in by her swift change of subject.

'You are not the same girl who came to St Lucien, Stephanie. You are either ill or it has been too much for you.'

'I told you,' Stephanie insisted, 'it was an adventure. Nobody could buy a holiday like that. It was fantastic. When it's all died down I'll be relating the tale to everyone for weeks on end.'

The dark eyes watched her steadily and then he shook his head, a slight smile on his face.

'Very well. If you say so but if you need us, Stephanie, all you have to do is call out and we'll be here.'

'You're a good brother-in-law,' Stephanie said softly. 'I can see why Fiona married you.'

'So can she—now!' He grinned at her, letting the subject of her health go. 'She is much better when kept under control and she is happier.'

'She looks it. I'm glad.' Stephanie smiled across at him and he smiled back knowingly.

'I have not actually been—what is the word? Sidetracked. I have merely decided to bide my time. When we return from St Lucien we shall come to see you at once. If you are not better by then I shall want to know the reason and I will not be put off.'

'Don't take your new role as master of the house too seriously,' Stephanie said warily. 'I'm only a relative by marriage.'

'In France,' he said proudly, 'we care for all our relatives. You are special too. You are my wife's sister and therefore, according to French custom, you come under my authority.'

'Do you want a fight?' Stephanie asked wryly and he was laughing again, back to being the Thierry she knew, although not exactly the same. He was stronger in every way and she wondered if it had been the shock of seeing Fiona injured and at the mercy of the elements or if it was Christian and some threat.

'I'm glad you're going to be with Jean-Paul,' she muttered.

'So am I. I have asked many times to be transferred to Paris, knowing that this day would come when Jean-Paul would go to a French school. Until now, though, Christian has ignored my requests. Perhaps he did not take me seriously, or perhaps I was not decisive enough.'

'Why has he transferred you now?' Stephanie asked and she got that shrug of the shoulders that instantly reminded her of Christian.

'Christian is getting married, or so I assume, because he informed me sharply that when he has children of his own he will be fully occupied.'

Stephanie's face went from hot to cold. Christian intended to marry and have a family of his own. The thought tore into her, making her feel ill, every dream dying completely. Just because he had been acting a part with Denise Pascal it did not mean that he had no one else. She knew nothing of his life.

'He—he'll be a difficult husband,' Stephanie murmured dully. She wanted to go away and cry but she had to go on facing Thierry.

'Probably,' Thierry said quietly. 'Are you happy, Stephanie?'

'Of course.' She managed to look bright but he eyed her quizzically. 'Why do you ask?'

'I am not blind. You are thin, *ma chère*, too slender, too pale.'

'Oh, I've had a cold,' she lied. 'Please don't mention it again, Thierry. I don't want Fiona fussing.'

Thierry let the whole matter drop but Stephanie felt he suspected that the cause of her slenderness was her time with Christian. She prayed he would say nothing. If he told Christian she was thin, pining away, she just couldn't bear it.

When they had gone she took a good look at herself for the first time and she saw what everyone else was seeing. She was over-slender, almost thin. There were dark marks beneath her eyes where there had been none before, no matter how late she had stayed up at night. Far from making her look older it made her look younger, as if she had not yet grown to any sort of maturity.

She would have to do something about it. She didn't exactly look like the photographs in her portfolio. When she went to these assignments they would be asking who she was. She almost didn't know that herself. She was what Christian had made her and her lips trembled as she thought of him being married, having children. She would never go to Paris, no matter how long Fiona and Thierry stayed there. She couldn't even go to see Jean-Paul.

Paris to her had now become Christian and she must never even catch a glimpse of him again as long as she lived or she would never be free. She had always felt free, happy and easygoing. Now she felt bereft, deserted. For some reason that she could not understand, Christian owned her. She loved him. Only her instinct to survive had prevented her from belonging to him completely.

CHAPTER TEN

STEPHANIE made herself go out the next morning. It would have been easy simply to stay around her flat and pine away for Christian but she had a life to live and sitting around dreaming about him would not help her to face things. The post had brought the schedule from her agent and she was not at all sure that she could fulfil it. All her energy seemed to have drained away.

She was just locking her front door when she looked up and saw a face she would rather not have seen at all.

'I was just coming to visit.' It was Rex Daniels, an actor she had known for some time. Originally he had pursued her quite relentlessly, dogging her footsteps and making quite a nuisance of himself. He was the sort of man who was completely sure of his own charm and normally Stephanie avoided him like the plague.

'What a pity,' she said, summoning up a smile. 'I'm just on my way out.'

He was not deterred—nothing much deterred him—and Stephanie just let it wash over her fatalistically. What did it matter anyway? It was somebody to talk to, somebody who would not mention Christian.

Her unusually submissive attitude merely brought out the ego in Rex and she found herself having lunch with him, a thing she had avoided with skill before. When he asked her to a party later she just agreed. It meant she would not be sitting in alone or wondering who to ring to take her mind off her miseries.

'I'll call for you at eight,' Rex told her smugly and she just nodded vaguely as she left him.

169

She walked home rather than take a taxi and she knew quite well that she was merely passing the time. How could she be so unhappy when not too long ago she had walked the same streets with a smile on her face? She had a lot of friends and she knew they would all turn up immediately if she called them. So would Fiona and Thierry. She didn't want any of them, though. She wanted Christian and it was rather like being sentenced to outer darkness.

Her mind seemed to be full of regrets. If only she had not spoken so cruelly. If only she had followed her heart and not her head. She kept remembering how Christian had held her and kissed her, the things he had said on that last night on the boat. And he had been quite right. She had fought him the more readily because she had felt drawn to him. Finally it was jealousy that had sharpened her tongue.

Getting ready was purely mechanical and she was surprised to see that she looked good. Her dress was a midnight-blue silk, very short, showing off her legs, and it clung to her figure almost lovingly. When she had her earrings on she felt a flicker of anxiety. Dressing like this had been a very thoughtless act and Rex was not entirely to be trusted at the best of times.

He rang the bell at that moment so changing was not an option and she quickly gathered her coat. She was not letting him in and her ready agreement to go out with him now seemed quite mad. She would have been better staying at home with her dreams.

'Well, well!'

She hated the way he looked her over and a bit of the spark came back into Stephanie's eyes. 'I assumed we were going to a smart place?' she said crisply, relieved to see that he was wearing a black tie.

'Would I be seen anywhere else?' Rex asked with a self-satisfied smile and Stephanie bit back sarcastic words. She had let herself be talked into this and she would have to see it out. Her nature made her see things through and she had agreed to come. It would be insulting to refuse now.

It was dark. Spring had not really arrived yet and Stephanie huddled inside her coat as they walked to his car. For a few minutes she had forgotten about Christian in her anxiety over this evening. Maybe it was a good sign? The trouble was that she didn't want to forget about him. She had tried that and been more unhappy than ever. It was like denying his existence. She would rather be unhappy with him in her head than not think about him at all.

By the time they reached the small West End hotel where the party was taking place, she had sunk back into her own world where she went over and over the time she had spent near Christian, clinging on to it almost frantically.

'I'll have to do something about you,' Rex said quite sourly after she had refused all drinks and danced with him in a purely automatic way. There were plenty of people there that she knew and although this had been quite a relief originally she had not been able to summon up the interest to speak to them for more than a few seconds.

Her gloomy face was deflating Rex's ego and he looked down at her a trifle grimly.

'I'm sorry,' Stephanie said, managing a smile. 'I don't seem to be able to get into things this evening.'

'That's soon taken care of.' He had manoeuvred her into a shadowy corner without her realising it and now he pulled her into his arms.

It spurred Stephanie into instant life.

'Let me go, Rex!' she said sharply. 'I can do without this sort of thing.'

'Don't be silly,' he laughed, holding her more tightly. 'I know you. You wouldn't have come out with me if you hadn't wanted to be close.'

'You invited me to a party,' Stephanie reminded him angrily, pushing to get free. 'I didn't have this sort of party in mind and if *you* had then you were mistaken. Let me go!'

He looked really ugly then, his face reddening with annoyance, and Stephanie was glad that there were other people within calling distance although she did not want the embarrassment of shouting for assistance. She was beginning to struggle rather frantically when someone appeared just behind Rex and the sight of him stilled Stephanie's struggles and sent every bit of colour from her face.

'Let her go!'

There was just the finest trace of a French accent in the voice and it was sheathed in ice. Rex spun round and found himself staring into blue eyes that promised murder. His arms fell away from Stephanie but he was too angry really to appreciate the danger.

'Keep out of this!' he snarled. 'She's with me! Who are you anyway? I know everyone here.'

'Let her go!' Christian's voice threatened menacingly. 'It will save me the trouble of killing you.'

Stephanie could hear the violence in his dark voice and she moved away quickly.

'Look, forget the whole thing, Rex...' she began in a trembling way but he was not in the mood to forget anything.

'Nobody scares me,' he snapped. 'This is none of his business. He's a gatecrasher. I want to know how he got in here.'

'I walked in,' Christian grated in a voice like silver ice. 'Now I intend to walk out.' He looked down at Stephanie with fury at the back of his brilliant eyes. 'Get your coat,' he ordered savagely.

She just moved off to obey but Rex made a grab for her arm, still determined to stop her. His hand never reached its destination because Christian gripped his arm with a ferocity that made him wince.

'Stephanie is with me,' he said with very quiet menace. 'Go back to your friends.'

The strength in that hand finally seemed to penetrate into Rex's mind because he pulled away irritably and after one bitter glance in Stephanie's direction he moved away.

'Now we leave. Collect your coat,' Christian ordered. He seemed to have even more anger in his voice and when she had her coat on the hand she knew from her dreams took her arm in an iron grip and she found herself out in the cool air, her feet only vaguely touching the pavement as Christian hurried her to his car.

'You'll get a ticket for parking here,' Stephanie said. She was feeling light-headed, not quite sure if she was dreaming, and he shot her a sideways glance like black lightning.

'You will be quiet until I get you home. After that you can explain to me just what you were doing with that man.'

'It—it was a party...'

'I could see the sort of party your friend had in mind!' he snapped. 'You are no more safe to be out on your own than you ever were. Be silent! You can spend the time thinking up some good excuses.'

She was in the luxury of Christian's car almost at once and she couldn't think of anything to say at all. He was here! Why was he here? Had he come to chastise her with the attitude that as she was vaguely related she should be kept under control? Had Thierry said something to him? As to how he had known where she was or how he knew where she lived, she couldn't fathom that out.

'How did you know where I was?' she asked after a minute when he simply drove with a grim look on his face.

'Fiona gave me your address and I arrived as you were leaving,' he grated. 'I followed you.'

'Why?' Stephanie asked in a whisper.

'I wished to speak to you. As things turned out it is as well. If that was a private party then it was not very secure. I simply walked in unchallenged. I had been standing at the bar since you arrived.'

'Spying on me,' Stephanie murmured, worried about how much he had seen of her misery.

'Watching you,' he corrected coolly. 'It is fortunate that I was there. You do not seem to be quite as capable of attacking enemies as you were before. Or perhaps he was not an enemy?'

'I—I just know him,' Stephanie explained and he grunted with annoyance.

'We will discuss this at your flat,' he ordered and Stephanie spun round in her seat to glare at him. She wanted him to hold her, to sweep her into his arms, but all he was doing was chastising her and he was cold as ice. Nothing had changed.

'I won't even let you *into* my flat!'

'I have never broken a door down,' he stated grimly. 'It will be a new experience.'

Stephanie didn't try saying anything after that. He was not about to listen and he certainly was not in the mood for answering questions. She didn't know what it all meant. He was behaving as if he had every right to act like this and she was really too stunned by his sudden arrival to defend herself at all.

She knew better than to try and shut him out of her flat but from the look on his face he half expected it.

'*Alors*!' he said sharply when they were inside and the door was locked. 'Now you may explain.'

'I have nothing to explain to you,' Stephanie informed him, knowing that she had to pull herself together or fall down and cry. 'I can't think why you're here and why you imagine you can tell me what to do.'

'I am here to see you, that is obvious,' he grated. He suddenly turned away, beginning to pace about, his eyes roaming over the room, and it seemed to Stephanie that he was disapproving.

'If you don't like my flat you needn't be in here,' she muttered, angry and anxious all at the same time.

'You are making rapid judgements again?' he enquired, turning to face her. 'The flat is attractive, tasteful and warm. I intend to stay. Shouting from a distance may be your way of conducting your affairs. It is not mine.'

'I just want to know why you've come,' Stephanie said desperately. She was finding it impossible to meet his gaze and now that he was simply standing and looking at her it was worse.

'Thierry came back to Paris yesterday and told me you were ill. According to my brother, I am to blame.'

'I never said that!' Stephanie looked at him with shocked eyes, her colour heightening and then paling again. 'I told him nothing at all. Why should he imagine . . . ?'

'I would think that your appearance was enough to make his imagination flourish,' Christian surmised, his eyes running over her as she stood and stared at him worriedly. 'What is this latest craze to become skin and bones? Did you make the decision yourself or have you been asked to do it for some magazine?'

'It—it's fashionable——' Stephanie began but he cut in on her words with his usual ruthless impatience.

'It is no such thing! It is impossible to improve on perfection. As far as I remember it was agreed that you are the most beautiful woman in the world. Knowing you, of course I can imagine you would have to try something new. As you are clearly losing your health at the same time I can quite see why Thierry was anxious.'

'It has nothing to do with you,' Stephanie said in a choked voice. 'It has nothing to do with Thierry either and just because he's suddenly become bossy he needn't think he's going to order me around and—and send you here to...'

'He did not send me here,' Christian assured her in a taut voice. 'I came of my own volition.' He stared at her, his face tightly controlled. 'Are you going to get changed from that tight, short dress?' he snapped. 'So far I have resisted the urge to tear it to pieces.'

Stephanie's face flooded with colour and she turned away abruptly.

'There's nothing wrong with this dress,' she faltered. 'It was very expensive. It suits me and—and anyway, I was at a party when you——'

'Yes, the party!' There was the suppressed violence back in his voice as he interrupted her. 'Who was the man who was pawing you?'

'It's just somebody I know,' Stephanie muttered. 'He invited me to the party and...'

'And decided to have a party of his own,' Christian rasped. 'You have a strange choice of boyfriends.'

'He's not a boyfriend.' Stephanie was beginning to feel as if she was backed into a corner and Christian was pinning her with eyes so blue and furious that she had trouble getting the next words out. 'I've always avoided him, but...' Her voice trailed away and Christian went very still.

'But you decided to go with him tonight, wearing that dress? Just how far would you have gone if I had not arrived, *mademoiselle*?'

'What exactly do you mean?' Stephanie flared, goaded into life at last. 'You have nothing to do with me. I can take care of myself and I would have done if you hadn't appeared so—so violently. And will you stop calling me *mademoiselle* in that superior tone? None of this is your affair.'

'Why did you go with him?' Christian persisted. 'I watched you for quite a while. You were not enjoying yourself. You were unhappy.'

'I wasn't in the mood,' Stephanie said crossly.

'Then why did you go?'

'Because I wanted to get out, because I just didn't care, because nothing matters!' she shouted.

Stephanie turned away abruptly. It was no use. He was just the same—angry, domineering. Why he was here she did not know unless he felt a duty towards her. She didn't want him to feel a duty. She wanted him to hold her and tell her that everything was all right.

'I'm sorry I shouted,' she said in a dull voice. 'I'm glad you came. I wanted to tell you that I regret speaking to you as I did. Once again, though, we're quarrelling.' She gave a long sigh. 'What does it matter? I'll get changed.'

'Why are you ill?' Christian was behind her, very close even though she had not heard him move, and Stephanie swallowed nervously.

'I'm not ill. I know I've lost a bit of weight but I expect it's the change of climate or something. It doesn't mean that I'm ill and even if I was...'

'Stephanie!' Christian warned darkly, taking her shoulders and turning her to face him. She couldn't face him, though. This was not at all how she had dreamed him. He was not here to say he had missed her. He was doing some sort of duty. She hung her head and when his hand tilted her face there were tears in her eyes.

'What is it, *ma belle*?' he asked gently. 'Why are you crying? I have frightened you with my anger?'

'I'm not frightened,' Stephanie gulped. 'Nothing frightens me and you should know that by now.' Tears escaped on to her cheeks and she pulled her face from his restraining fingers. 'If you came to frighten me...'

'*Mon Dieu*. I came to see you. I *had* to see you. When Thierry said you looked ill I could not even sleep.' He captured her face again, cupping it in his hands. 'Tell me the truth! Why do you look like this? Why do you cry when I have done enough, said enough, to have my Stephanie throwing heavy objects at me?'

She just stared at him through her tears, suddenly noticing how strained he looked. He had called her his Stephanie. Did he mean it? Was it just a mistake?

'I missed you,' she whispered. 'I—I don't seem to want to eat any more. Nothing is the same. You even get into my dreams,' she finished fretfully, looking up at him with a spark of her old anger showing through the tears. And Christian was smiling down at her, reaching for her.

'I counted on your courage, *chérie*,' he said softly. 'I prayed that you would dare to tell me the truth.' His arms closed tightly round her and he began to kiss away her tears with an urgency that told her he too was desperate to be close. 'I have missed you too,' he murmured between kisses. 'I have longed for you every day. And if how you are now is the result of my neglect, I will keep you close, never allow you out of my sight. I will never let you leave me again.'

'You didn't try to keep me before,' Stephanie reminded him, still sobbing although she wound her arms round his neck.

'How could I?' he whispered against her face. 'I spent my time on St Lucien trying to keep my distance from you. I had a part to play with Denise and I knew that if I allowed my feelings for you to show she would be alerted to the fact that I knew who she was.' He bent his head and looked into her eyes when Stephanie winced at the name. 'I did not make love to her, *chérie*,' he assured her softly. 'It is true that I was obliged to kiss her and hold her, to let her think that her plan was succeeding, but do not imagine that things ever went further than that. I was you I wanted to be with in the night.'

'Why didn't you tell me?' Stephanie said plaintively, shivering at the seductive sound of his voice, and he shook his head, gathering her closer to him.

'At first I could not. Your face would have given everything away. You are not too good at hiding your thoughts. Later, I had to let you go.'

'Why?' Stephanie demanded pitifully. 'Why did you have to? You could tell how I felt and I've been so unhappy.'

'Don't, *mon ange*,' he pleaded. 'The things you said to me assured me that I was mistaken about how you felt. You accused me of so many things and I told myself that if you cared about me you would have trusted me. I thought then that the way you reacted to me was just that you had been part of an adventure, part of the excitement. I thought that you would return to London and take up your life as before. It was only when Thierry told me that you looked ill and unhappy that I dared to hope.'

'Thierry says you're going to have a family,' Stephanie said miserably, suddenly remembering and trying to pull away from his arms. 'Are you getting married?' She still did not know how things worked in his wealthy world.

'If you will agree to be the bride,' he murmured, trailing teasing fingers along her neck and shoulders. 'I cannot have my silver-haired children unless you are their mother.'

Stephanie gasped as his gently exploring fingers moved beneath the neckline of her dress to seek the rose-tipped mounds of her breast and his mouth covered hers in a searching, demanding kiss. Her whole body began to melt as his fingers caressed the quickly swelling nipples and she moaned softly, almost dissolving into him, her lips open beneath his and his insistence grew.

'Now can I hold you against me in the night and prove how much I love you?' he asked thickly against her mouth. 'Can I show you how sweet things will be between us, my Stephanie?'

'Oh, yes!' Stephanie's head fell back as his mouth moved hotly on her skin and he swept her up into his arms, moving unerringly with her to the bedroom.

'I wish that this were my bed,' he told her unevenly. 'I wish that the first time and the rest of our lives would be in my bed.'

'It's chauvinistic,' Stephanie whispered in a shaken voice as he put her down and looked at her with burning blue eyes.

'It is how I am. It is how I feel about you. I wanted you with a frightening desperation right from the first.'

He came down to her, undressing her quickly, holding her against him when he too was undressed, and Stephanie curled herself into him, still dazed by the way he had come almost in answer to her dreams.

'I thought I would never see you again,' she whispered. 'I thought you were getting married. I couldn't bear it.'

'And I thought you would forget me,' he countered almost angrily, kissing her fiercely. 'You were mine and I could not claim you. Tonight I thought you had gone back to your old life. You were with people I did not know. You were with another man and wearing a dress that made my heart stop!' He suddenly relaxed, his touch more gentle. 'But I looked at your face in the light and saw how pale you were, how those lovely eyes had lost their sparkle. You have been pining for me, *chérie*, hmm?'

'All the time,' she choked. 'I even imagined I saw you but it was never you.'

'Shh. I am here now.' His eyes swept over her and he smiled. 'We will see what happens to this interesting slenderness after a few nights in my arms. Tomorrow I will take you home, to my house and my bed. I have dreamed every night that you were there beside me.'

His mouth sought hers, fierce and insistent as his fingers tangled in her hair, and as he moved down her body, placing heated kisses on every part of her skin, Stephanie cried out in excitement, twisting beneath him as an ache grew inside her that she remembered only too well.

'I love you, Christian,' she gasped, urging him closer.

'I know, my sweetest Stevie,' he groaned. 'I know now. If I had known before, these miserable weeks without you would not have almost killed me.'

'Please!' she begged when everything inside her was yearning to be part of him and he moved over her quickly, his lips closing over hers as he possessed her. The pain was sharp but brief and Stephanie was too committed to belonging to him to protest. She relaxed against him and he took her to another world that was wonder and light, colour and distant sound.

When she spiralled back to earth he was watching her with smiling eyes, tenderness on his face.

'Is it always like that?' she asked breathlessly, still clinging to him.

'With you I suspect it will always be like that,' he murmured gently. 'You are part of me. You have been part of my heart since I saw you.'

'You hated me!' Stephanie protested, cuddling against him when he moved and lay watching the ceiling.

'I hated myself,' he corrected her ruefully. 'I thought I was looking at a teenager and I was shocked to find that I wanted you. Even when I knew you were older than you looked, the impression remained and I felt a good deal of guilt. It was only when you appeared dressed as a grown-up woman that I breathed a sigh of relief.'

'It didn't do a lot to change your attitude,' Stephanie grumbled and he slanted a blue-eyed look of amusement at her.

'You expected it to change? You took more looking after than Jean-Paul. I had Denise spying round every corner, I had Jean-Paul to protect and I never knew what you would do at any time. I was afraid for you. It was decidedly tricky,' he muttered, tightening his arm around her waist.

'I still can't see why we didn't just all go to the *Sea Queen*,' she protested.

'I had told Denise that the yacht had returned to Fort-de-France. She was under the impression that we were at the house with no sort of help. If she had known of the *Sea Queen* she would have warned the others and they would not have been caught so easily. When you injured my men, however, I decided that she had probably been watching the episode and that no useful purpose would be served by waiting for events to overtake us. I got rid of her and hoped that the police would pick up the others as they arrived and stop them from communicating with her.'

'When she came, I thought she was your mistress. She was on the *Sea Queen* with you.'

'I had no intention of letting her out of my sight,' Christian stated grimly. 'They have succeeded well before because of the information that some woman like Denise has been able to pass on. On board the yacht she could do nothing at all. She had no means of communicating with them. That was how the police were able to get them. That was why they walked into the trap.'

'Only two, though,' Stephanie reminded him and he nodded in agreement.

'I only expected two. I know their methods. Firstly someone worms their way into the household. Sometimes it is as a maid, sometimes, as with Denise, as an attractive woman to insinuate herself into the life of the intended target. Various women have been used. I had never known of Denise before but I was expecting it. Two would be left in France or wherever they had decided to operate. When I was sure that the two had been arrested on St Lucien, I merely had to await word from France. Then I was able to take Denise back to Paris.'

'It was a shock,' Stephanie told him seriously and he laughed without much humour.

'It was certainly a shock to her. By that time they had all been caught.'

'She was in your bedroom,' Stephanie said slowly, still a little worried by that episode.

'Do you trust me, Stephanie?' he asked, moving to look down at her, and she looked back into the wonderful blue eyes and smiled.

'Yes. I've always trusted you, I suppose. I fought you but I relied on you and I was terrified that you would be hurt.' She looked up at him thoughtfully. 'But she was in your room all the same.'

'I don't doubt it. I never did. I can only surmise that she was, once again, spying. She was never in my room when I was there.'

'I know,' Stephanie said, covering his face with kisses. 'Looking back,' she mused when he had stopped her with kisses of his own, 'I didn't help much.'

'But you made a very big impression, *chérie*.' He smiled down into her thoughtful face. 'I have two men who will now give serious consideration to wearing sunglasses whenever they are near to sand. I have a captain who is still dazzled by your beauty and I have a crew who will often look up at the rigging on the slight chance that you will be stuck up there.'

'You're saying that I made a hash of things?'

'Whatever that means,' he agreed, 'I probably am. It was not all disaster, however. I held you and kissed you and you taught me to look round corners in case anyone should be waiting there to assault me.' He grinned into her dark eyes and then gathered her close to him. 'You taught me to be madly in love,' he whispered, beginning to kiss her again. 'What did I teach you?'

'I'm not sure. I'll tell you soon,' Stephanie said shakily.

'What happened to Fiona?' Stephanie asked later when they were lying contentedly in each other's arms. 'She seemed to be different.'

'For now,' Christian agreed. 'Thierry appears to have taken charge. I suppose it was the accident.'

'You said that he'd made a mistake in marrying Fiona,' Stephanie reminded him. 'You threatened to intervene.'

'I was hurting, *chérie*,' he sighed. 'You had just shown that you did not love me and in my misery I said many things that I did not believe.'

Stephanie wrapped her arms round him and kissed his cheek.

'I'll never hurt you again,' she whispered. 'I didn't know I could hurt you.'

'Nobody else can, only you.' He looked happy again and she hesitated to bring up anything else that was contentious. Christian answered her unspoken question.

'I did not intend to make Jean-Paul my responsibility,' he assured her. 'Many times Thierry has asked to be moved to Paris and every time Fiona has complained. I needed to force her hand.'

Stephanie began to laugh, remembering that Fiona had intended to get the better of Christian. When he looked at her enquiringly, she told him about Fiona's plan.

'She's met her match at last,' Stephanie pointed out with a wide smile when he looked startled. 'All the same,' she said dreamily, 'it will be wonderful seeing her more often. We'll all be living in Paris and I'll have time for Jean-Paul.'

'Not much time,' Christian murmured seductively. 'You will have children of your own. Jean-Paul will have many silver-haired cousins. It will keep both of you out of mischief.'

*   *   *

Stephanie and Jean-Paul stood at the long window in Christian's elegant house just outside Paris and watched the snow fall silently, the heavy flakes coating the garden with magic. It was almost Christmas and Jean-Paul was staying with them for a few days.

'It is fantastic!' he said in an awestricken voice. 'I have never seen snow before in the whole of my life. Shall we go out and run about in it, Stevie?'

'You shall not!' Christian put down his paper and came to stand by them, his arm around Stephanie. 'Stevie is in no condition to race about the garden.' His hand came protectively to the swollen mound of her stomach and Stephanie leaned against him with a sigh of contentment.

'When my cousin is born,' Jean-Paul announced importantly, 'I will teach him *everything*.'

'He may be a girl,' Stephanie pointed out and he looked at her seriously.

'I would not mind. You have always been a girl and you are more fun than any of the boys at school. They seem to me to be afraid of adventures. If my new cousin is like you, it will be good enough.'

He turned back to watching the snow, pressing his nose against the pane.

'There is nothing to stop you from going out there by yourself,' Christian pointed out wryly. 'You are not attached to your aunt by a chain.'

'I will go,' Jean-Paul said excitedly, adding with a frown, 'But it will not be much fun without Stevie.'

'Nothing is much fun without Stevie,' Christian told her softly when Jean-Paul had gone, 'and I am very grateful that you are a girl.'

Stephanie wound her arms around his neck and looked up at him with starry eyes.

'Do you want a boy or a girl?' she asked dreamily. 'You never say.'

'I never say because I do not mind,' he murmured, bending his dark head to kiss her. 'I want you. Children are a bonus and making them is happiness but my life is entwined around you and it always will be.'

'I might never have met you,' Stephanie sighed and Christian's arms tightened round her at once.

'Don't even think things like that,' he murmured. 'My life would have been empty.'

'With Fiona and Thierry in Paris I would have been sure to meet you, I expect,' Stephanie mused, 'although I wouldn't have been as infuriating as I was on the island and you might not have been interested.'

'Interested?' Christian laughed, dropping a kiss on her lips. 'I can see that you have taken to making understatements. I cannot even think of words to describe how I have felt about you since I first saw you. Interested, however, is not a word I would have chosen.'

'I still manage to get into trouble,' she reminded him ruefully.

'You seem to be thriving on it,' he murmured, glancing at her flushed cheeks. She cuddled against him, remembering how unhappy she had been. Now Christian's love was all around her and every day was filled with joy.

'Our nephew is occupied,' he whispered against her ear as André came out to join Jean-Paul in the garden. 'You should have your afternoon rest and I should be with you.' His hand covered her swollen breasts and his face softened as his eyes moved over her possessively. 'My beautiful Stevie,' he said gently. 'I love you so much.'

Stephanie looked up into the brilliant blue eyes, her face alive with happiness. His lips closed over hers and everything else just faded away. She was in a world of her own with Christian, the feeling of destiny real at last. It had been there when she was nineteen and watching him secretly. If she had known then that the wonder she felt, the almost shivering awareness, had been because she had seen her future she would not have believed it. Now she knew and nothing but happiness stretched before her.

HARLEQUIN ROMANCE®

brings you

The written word has played an important role in all our romances in our Sealed With a Kiss series so far and next month's #3378 *Angels Do Have Wings* by Helen Brooks is no exception.

But just as Angel Murray was writing a long letter to her best friend explaining that nothing exciting ever happened to her—something did. A rich, tall and utterly gorgeous stranger walked into her life and casually turned it upside down.

What could a man like Hunter Ryan possibly want with a girl like her? Despite the attraction that flared between them, they were worlds apart. Angel could never reconcile herself to a temporary affair and that was clearly all he was offering her. But Hunter's charm was proving all too persuasive. And as for his kiss...

From the celebrated author of
And the Bride Wore Black.

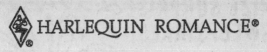

HARLEQUIN ROMANCE®

brings you

Romances that take the family to heart!

#3377 FOREVER ISN'T LONG ENOUGH
by Val Daniels

In one rash moment Mark Barrington had told his sick father that he was engaged to a truly wonderful girl. A white lie designed to make his father's dreams come true—after all, all his Pop wanted in life was to see his son safely settled down and, of course, meet the woman in question! And that was the problem—Mark need a fiancée and he needed one fast!

Sarah Fields could have been made to order! She had just lost her job, and Mark had appeared on the horizon like the proverbial white knight in a fairy tale, offering her a rather unusual post as his prospective bride. But for Sarah there was just one difficulty with this make-believe romance—the magic couldn't last forever!

Coming next month, from the bestselling author of *Silver Bells!*

FT-4

PRIZE SURPRISE SWEEPSTAKES!

This month's prize:

BEAUTIFUL WEDGWOOD CHINA!

This month, as a special surprise, we're giving away a bone china dinner service for eight by Wedgwood**, one of England's most prestigious manufacturers!

Think how beautiful your table will look, set with lovely Wedgwood china in the casual Countryware pattern! Each five-piece place setting includes dinner plate, salad plate, soup bowl and cup and saucer.

The facing page contains two Entry Coupons (as does every book you received this shipment). Complete and return *all* the entry coupons; **the more times you enter, the better your chances of winning!**

Then keep your fingers crossed, because you'll find out by September 15, 1995 if you're the winner!

Remember: The more times you enter, the better your chances of winning!*

*NO PURCHASE OR OBLIGATION TO CONTINUE BEING A SUBSCRIBER NECESSARY TO ENTER. SEE THE REVERSE SIDE OF ANY ENTRY COUPON FOR ALTERNATE MEANS OF ENTRY.

**THE PROPRIETORS OF THE TRADEMARK ARE NOT ASSOCIATED WITH THIS PROMOTION.

PWW KAL